# The House in the Mountains

**This Short Story collection is a compilation of gripping tales in English and German from the Swiss Mountains, playing out in the same alpine region, in the same dwelling.**

The stories can be read independent of each other.

I dedicate these stories to my mum who lived in the mountains and loved reading short stories. She would have been able to read them in both languages as she went to English lessons right into old age.

A heartfelt thanks to my favourite writers: Thomas Hardy, Amelia B. Edwards, Susan Hill, Jeremias Gotthelf, Thomas Mann and many more.

# THE HOUSE IN THE MOUNTAINS

## The Return

After an hour's climb from the valley, Anna reached the village of Untersee. She shrugged the wooden carrier into a more comfortable position. Her shoulders hurt from the heavy load. She tugged at the stiff collar of her dress, unbuttoned the twill coat and pulled the skirts away from much-darned stockings. Strands of ginger hair clung to her face.

The village square of Untersee was deserted. Anna passed the church; its whitewash gleamed in the afternoon sun. With a hasty sign of the cross, she asked God to forgive her for not stopping and saying a prayer.

'Napoleon,' she whispered, 'come here, good dog.' Holding on to the scruff of his neck, she hurried past the houses and barns. Scrunching up her face, she looked straight ahead, as if this would make her invisible. Meeting any of the locals would only lead to awkward questions.

As she rushed past the last dwelling, a voice called out, 'Anna Imholz, wait.'

Anna stopped dead. She knew that voice. Hans was one of the few boys from this village who had attended school lessons at the rectory down in the small county town where she lived with her family. They had stayed on friendly terms, and every time she had seen him at the market, they had exchanged a few words.

Hans gripped her arm. 'I saw you and your father bring down the cows from the Alp. What are you doing heading back up there? Now in autumn!'

'I am going back to Obsee to wait for Peter,' Anna replied.

Catching hold of her wooden carrier, Hans removed it from her back. 'I'll come with you. I've nothing better to do.' He pulled the canvas straps over his shoulders, and they set off.

Hans kicked at a stone. 'I... I have heard, there were heavy casualties on both sides, in the battles for Lombardy. If Peter... if any of the Swiss mercenaries survived, they'd be back by now.'

Anna's steps slowed; she tried to keep upright. It couldn't be. How dare Hans speculate? Her husband was alive. He had promised to be back before winter and to return from the campaign a rich man. They would buy a farm in the lowlands of Switzerland and start a family.

She tousled Napoleon's fur and wiped away tears of frustration. Peter had given her the dog as a keepsake.

Anna and Hans walked through the gorge, the cliffs closing in on them. Fallen trees and damp rocks filled the air with the smell of death and decay. Napoleon, as large as a calf, led the way. He ran far ahead only to race back, making sure they were catching up.

Hans, strong and sure-footed, adjusted the carrier every so often. Anna, at the rear, climbed the rough stone steps cut into the sheer cliffs with ease.

When they came out of the gorge, they saw two eagles swooping in and out of the rocky fissures above them, their eerie cries echoing around the cliffs.

The path divided: one track curved down into a neighbouring valley, another led across a field of scree. It would be difficult to walk; jagged and slippery with the glutinous substance of rotten vegetation and water springing from between pieces of slate. Deep below them, a thin ribbon of melted glacier-ice snaked its way through giant boulders.

'I'll be fine from here. It'll take me half an hour or so,' Anna said. She didn't want Hans to come any further and see the repairs that needed doing to the hut after the first autumn storm. He would be bound to climb onto the roof, replace the missing tiles, and insist on re-hanging the shutters. All these jobs she could do herself.

Impatiently she pulled at the carrier, making Hans topple backward.

'Hang on, easy does it.' He lowered the carrier to the ground, and she crouched down, leaning against its wooden ladder back. She slipped the broad straps over her shoulders, slowly getting up while trying to find a foothold on the loose shingle. Hans took hold of her, his strong hands on her hips, his face hovering above hers. She pushed him away.

'You'll starve,' Hans said. 'The winter up there is hard. Why don't you stay with your father down in the valley and wait there?'

'Peter will be back before the first snowfall. Father left the goats, so I have milk, and I'll make cheese.' Anna pointed to the carrier. 'I bought flour and sugar. There's plenty of wood. I can bake bread, and I have books to read. No need to worry.'

'I'll come to see you. Be hunting up in the cliffs as soon as the snow freezes over.'

'Thank you, God bless,' Anna called after him.

Having crossed the field of scree and emerging from the thicket of larches, Anna gave a loud yodel. She would never tire of this view. Before her lay a vast plateau surrounded by sheer cliffs rising to snow-covered peaks. The glacier lake glittered in the golden glow of the late afternoon sun. At its far end, the alpine hut sat in a grassy meadow, behind it a stand of fir swayed gently in the breeze.

Between boulders, a narrow track wound its way up to the pass. There Peter had left, and there he would return before the lake froze over and snow buried the hut. Together they would climb down into the valley and stay with her family until spring.

Anna settled into a routine. The low raftered room where she spent most of her waking hours provided all she needed: a cavernous fireplace, a table with two rickety chairs, and a built-in dresser. In the hayloft, she slept on a thick layer of straw. Jute sacks stuffed with dried leaves served as a cover and pillow.

Rising with the first sign of dawn, she put on her boots and stepped down into the barn to milk the two goats. Back in the hut, she filled a bowl with milk, added pieces of bread and a handful of oats for Napoleon. A kettle with water hung over the fire. Coffee was her only luxury. Turning the handle of the coffee grinder, she hummed a tune.

Once a week, she poured the goats' milk into the cauldron and stirred until it curdled. The curds she shaped into flavoursome cheese rounds. Baking loaves of bread every so often had become a ritual. She collected the last of the blueberries and made jam. She wanted to be ready for her husband's return.

Later, when all the work was done, she sat by the window and read the Bible. She felt bad not going to church on Sundays but reading the Old and New Testament quietened her conscience.

The days grew shorter, and she climbed the ladder to the hayloft as soon as the light faded. The wind shook the hut making it into a living thing, a companion talking to her. She listened to its beams sigh and floorboards groan. In the stable, she heard the occasional bleat of the goats.

One morning Anna tried to open the shutters, but they were stuck fast, as was the door. Snow had fallen overnight; the wind had grown into a blizzard, snowdrifts imprisoned her. She put extra logs into the open hearth, sending sparks up the chimney. For a moment, it went pitch-dark, and she panicked. She was buried alive.  Then the wood caught and lit the room in a golden glow. It took all her strength to clear the snow from doors and windows.

Peter was never far from her thoughts. Before going to sleep, pictures of him in his blue uniform, handsome and brave, crowded her mind. She dreamt of the battles Peter fought in Napoleon's army. Together with hundreds of soldiers, he advanced across the vast plains of Lombardy, bayonets at the ready. Running after him, she was unable to catch up. Every time, she woke up bathed in sweat and trembling.

Once a week, she stripped off her clothes to have a snow bath. She had grown so thin. Large blue veins crisscrossed her legs, and her arms were like sticks. She no longer believed in herself, in her ability to survive up here. Because of the sparse feed, the goats' milk had dried up. Was it one or two months since she had started rationing food? Napoleon was fine; he hunted snow rabbits and got his fill.

Was she waiting in vain? Was Hans right? If Peter had survived the battles, he would have returned before the winter. She shook herself. No, she could not give up on him; he was not going to let her down.

Anna had whittled a calendar of thirty days on one of the wooden beams. With a piece of charred wood, she crossed off a number every day. Christmas had come and gone. If she counted right, it was the beginning of February. It would be spring soon.

Heavy snowfalls made her a prisoner, but whenever possible, she dragged herself through the waist-deep snow so she could see the pass. She stared and willed Peter to appear between the cliffs. She could see a speck getting larger coming across the field of ice ever closer and eventually hugging her to his broad chest, no longer dressed in uniform but in an old coat, a battered hat pulled over his dark hair. He was used to all weathers. For him, coming over the pass was child's play. Every day she waited and prayed for his safe arrival.

One day she heard something scrape at the door. There it was again, scraping, then a metallic clink. The door opened slowly.

'Peter... he's back.' Anna's heart raced. She ran to the door and pulled it open.

Hans stepped into the hut, and with him came a blast of ice-cold air. Flushed and out of breath, he put his hunting rifle behind the door and shrugged off his rucksack and coat.

'You... it's only you?' Anna said.

Coughing, she tried to remove the lump in her throat. After a while, there was a new spring in her step. She bustled around, humming, talking and slicing the last loaf of bread and the final round of cheese. She put more logs on the fire and ground coffee. It was good to have someone to talk to, another human to look at.

Sitting on the one-legged milking stool by the open hearth, Hans listened to Anna's chatter, whittling a piece of wood.

'You were right, it's not easy, a whole winter up here. But see, I managed.' Anna pulled herself up and pushed out her chin. 'There was no time to brood. I kept busy doing repairs to the hut, making cheese, baking bread, and many other chores. Freeing the hut every time it snowed was a never-ending job.'

She handed Hans a mug of coffee and gave him a challenging look. 'Peter will come back. I know. You… you… don't tell me otherwise!'

He shook his head. 'No, no, they're dead, all of them. They've long been buried in the fields of Lombardy.'

Anna stared at him and wiped a hand across her eyes. Waiting for her husband had been nothing but a vigil for a man long dead.

Hans stayed all afternoon, and when night came, they climbed up into the hayloft together.

The first rays of a wintry sun streamed through the skylight when Anna woke. She heard a noise, rusty hinges grating, and the excited yelp of Napoleon, steps on the floorboards. The rungs of the ladder creaked. Silence! The door banged shut. She lay there, paralysed. Beside her, under the jute sack, she could make out a shape. Hans muttered in his sleep. Horrified, she put her hands to her face.

In her nightdress, she climbed down the ladder. Snow clung to the rungs. There was no sign of Napoleon. Peter! Peter! She wanted to shout, but no sound came. Peter was the only person the dog would have gone with. She sank to the floorboards and ran her fingers over the snow-encrusted footprints.

Tortured with guilt and fear, she lost track of time. How long had she been there on her knees doing penance, minutes, a quarter of an hour or longer? Again and again, she banged her head against the wood. Her hands trembled, and her legs shook. Like an old woman, she pulled herself up, clinging to the wall. She tore open the door and ran barefoot into the snow, following the footprints, oblivious of the pain in her feet.

Two black figures, a man and a dog, moved across the field of snow, steadily, inexorably, away from her, towards the pass.

Falling into the snow, she clawed at it. What had she done? All winter, she had waited for Peter, and one moment of recklessness had destroyed everything. She screamed a wounded animal's scream.

She dragged herself back to the hut. Hans had gone. Shivering she put the last of the logs on the fire.

Kneeling in front of the roaring blaze, she rocked back and forth, her hands over her ears.

Later, much later, she got up, packed her carrier, untied the goats and like a ghost, wandered with them down into the valley.

## A Christmas Ghost Story

'Wake up, Niklaus! You're to go with Father Stockman up to Obsee. He's taking communion to Imholz Sepp and will give him his last rites.'

Mother's voice faded in and out. Niklaus tried to focus and pull himself out of a deep slumber. It was Christmas Eve and after all the excitement of the celebrations the heat of the stove had lulled him to sleep.

Niklaus's body ached as he pulled on his boots, the sheepskin jerkin, gloves, and woollen hat his mother held ready.

'You'll make it before Midnight Mass if you hurry. One hour there, one hour back.'

Mother took holy water from the ceramic stoup hanging by the door and made the sign of the cross on his forehead. 'The foresters have been bringing back the logs from up there; the snow is compacted, the going shouldn't be too bad.'

By now, Niklaus was fully awake, and it came to him that this was a vital mission, for without the last rites no man could enter the Kingdom of Heaven. He squared his shoulders, and his eyes lit up. From all the altar boys, Father Stockman had chosen him.

The dying man, Sepp Imholz, lived on the alp Obsee even in the winter.  It was the most isolated homestead in the whole county, in no man's land, nobody knew if it was part of the parish of Untersee or the parish of Melchtal.

The priest waited for Niklaus at the portal of the church and handed him the lantern and the brass vessel with the holy oil. Dressed in his black cassock and velvet cape, he carried the communion in a small silver monstrance. He was young, fresh from the seminary and didn't know his parish well.

'We have to get a move on; Sepp Imholz is dying. His neighbour knocked on my door not thirty minutes ago and told me to hurry.'

Niklaus shrugged his shoulders. Sepp didn't have any neighbours.

An icy wind blew from the east as they headed through the village towards the river gorge. Ice crunched under their feet. It started to snow. Big wet flakes landed on the lantern, sparkled and melted. Niklaus's gloves were soggy in no time. Icy water trickled down his neck. He was freezing.

In the gorge, it was warmer; the towering cliffs provided shelter. The air was full of strange noises; the Melchibach, deep down, sucked and gurgled, Father Stockman murmured the rosary, and night animals scurried into their hideouts. Niklaus remembered his grandmother telling him that on Christmas Eve the dead get a chance to come back and make good the things they'd neglected to do. He fancied that the souls of the departed were swishing past him on important errands.

Coming out of the gorge, they climbed the steep slope towards the plateau.

Father Stockman wasn't used to the mountainous terrain. 'Not so fast, young Niklaus,' he shouted.

Niklaus slowed down, turned and waited for the priest who had gathered his cassock with one hand and tried to hold on to the monstrance with the other. Like a fish out of water, he gasped for air.

The larches swayed above them, and a half-moon appeared between heavy clouds. It had stopped snowing, but from the branches of the trees, small shards of icicles rained down.

Climbing on to the plateau, they saw the dwelling standing black and squat in the snowy landscape. No smoke came from the chimney. Like skeletal fingers, the fir trees, behind the cabin, pointed into an inky sky. The small lake had frozen solid. It was difficult to tell if they walked on ice or the snowy path.

Niklaus set down the lantern on the water trough and slipped out of his gloves. His hands were frozen, his toes ached, and his lungs were bursting from the walk in the freezing air. Father caught up with him and pushed at the door. It opened with a grating sound. Niklaus lit the way through the large low raftered room, the lantern painting eerie shadows on the flagstone floor. Above him, on a beam, he made out carvings that looked like numbers - perhaps days of the months.

A door swung open, as if by a ghost's hand. The floorboards creaked as they stepped into the room at the back. Father started praying, 'Bless this dwelling and all who live in it,' and made the sign of the cross.

Niklaus stayed at the foot of the bed. A draft made the door crash shut, the candle in the lantern guttered and went out plunging the room in darkness. Niklaus's stomach somersaulted, and his skin crawled with what seemed thousands of tiny spiders. Through the grimy window, he saw a cloud reveal the moon. A beam of light crept across the eiderdown, illuminating a white face. Black sockets stared towards the ceiling, claw-like fingers held the sheet. Imholz Sepp had been ill for some time and had changed from a rotund, jolly red-faced man to a mere skeleton.

Father Stockman said the necessary prayers, anointed the dying man with oil and put the communion wafer into his toothless, gaping mouth. Holding his hand, he beckoned Niklaus to do the same. Reluctantly he obeyed and took hold of the skinny fingers but withdrew quickly. They were cold, so cold.

Father had to celebrate midnight Mass, so they couldn't stay.

Returning ten minutes before twelve, Niklaus and the priest entered the church through the vestry door. The organ was playing O Come, All Ye Faithful, and a quick look from behind the altar confirmed that the candle-adorned benches were packed with worshippers. Niklaus pulled the red vestment, held up by the sacristan, over his head.

The Mass ended with the Christmas carol of Silent Night. Father Stockman stood at the door of the church, busy shaking hands with the parishioners. Niklaus joined his parents to wish their priest a happy Christmas.

Tante Emma, the village gossip, shouldered Niklaus and his parents out of the way. She knew everything: who was born and who had died, who had been up to mischief and who had been charitable. Father shook her hand.

Her headscarf slipped from her thinning grey hair and she pronounced, 'So Imholz Sepp passed away. I've heard that his funeral in Melchtal was some days ago. It's so sad he'd never sent for you to give him last rites.' She wiped a tear from her parchment face.

Father's face turned the colour of snow covering the church steps. Niklaus took his mother's hand. So Sepp had been buried some days ago. But he had seen him clearly two hours, or so, ago. He'd even touched his hand. A shudder ran down Niklaus's spine.

Remembering Grandmother's story, Niklaus concluded that it was Sepp's ghost he'd seen, taking advantage of the hours of grace on Christmas Eve. He had died without a priest, condemning him to walk the glaciers forever, but then he was allowed to rise from his grave to fetch Father to give him his last rites.

Out of the corners of his eyes, Niklaus watched Father. How would he deal with this situation? The priest slowly pulled himself up to his full height, looked at his congregation and thundered, 'Of course, Sepp's had his last rites, isn't that so, Niklaus, didn't we go up to Obsee for exactly that purpose?'

Niklaus nodded and stammered, 'Y - yep, we did.'

Like Father, he kept quiet about the exact time or day. Niklaus head felt light and he could have sworn that, amongst the people, he had spotted a pale, thin face and a parched mouth widening into a smile.

## The Pilgrimage

On one side, the post bus hugged the cliffs and trickles of water obscured the glass. On the other, the wheels teetered at the edge of the road, the land falling away down to where the Melchibach rushed its way through a narrow gorge. Farmhouses clung to grassy slopes, now mid-morning, still in deep shadow. Steep pine forests led up to craggy cliffs and fields of scree and snow. Granite mountain peaks towered towards a cerulean sky.

Paul and a woman in a flowery dress were the only passengers travelling to the village of Untersee. She stared at him but Paul was sure that nobody would recognise him, not after so many years. To the villagers he would be the typical elderly tourist, in corduroy trousers and check shirt, walking in the mountains.

He rubbed his eyes and stretched his arms.

Gravel hit the chassis. Paul jumped. He wiped the window with the back of his sleeve. On this road, he had walked flat out, forty years ago, all the way down to the railway station to catch the steam train to Lucerne. From there he had travelled on to Rotterdam and boarded a ship bound for the Promised Land. His few belongings he carried in a burlap sack. Canada had beckoned a farm on the vast plains of Manitoba. He'd had a rocky start, first working as a stable hand, then building up his own business growing wheat. Now his sons had taken over. His wife was dead, and he was no longer needed.

Queasy from tortuous hairpin bends, Paul breathed a sigh of relief when the bus pulled into the village square. He grabbed his knapsack and walking stick and descended, nodding a thank you to the driver. A sleepy dog on the steps of one of the chalets raised his head, a few chickens pecked at the gravel, and an old lady, wearing a headscarf, hastened towards the church, muttering a Grüezi.

Paul's eyes swept up to the dark evergreen forests, the alpine meadows, waterlogged cliffs, the fields of eternal snow, and craggy pinnacles. He opened his arms as if to embrace all of it. In the Canadian praries the horizon was without limit, nothing but sky. Here the mountains were the masters; you had to conquer them to see the firmament. His throat tightened and his eyes burned. How he had missed all of this.

The cobbled alleyway, lined by dark, weather-beaten chalets, led him past the whitewashed church. He crossed himself. The village was deserted, only from the schoolhouse came signs of life; the children chanted their times' tables.

A small wooden house came into view. Paul wiped a hand across his forehead and muttered, 'Thank you, God.' He was glad that it hadn't been modernised with cheap replacement windows and a new facade. Nothing had changed; the tiny lead windows were intact, the beams still looked weathered and split, the overhanging roof had a few shingles missing, and some of the shutters could have done with a lick of paint.

None of his family lived here now. Mother and Father were buried in the county town's cemetery and his brother had moved to Zürich.

It was early. Paul decided that he would go up to Obsee, the alp he had inherited. He had been lucky his brother had found a long-term tenant - his name escaped him. The dwelling, after all these years, would be in a bad state of repair. Passed down over generations, nobody had ever done anything with it, and the pastures were used for cattle grazing only.

A sharp breeze had sprung up. Here in the mountains, storms came from the west, always. Paul watched the billowing clouds over the Rotstock. Tendrils of mist had begun to envelop the bottom of the cliffs. He hesitated. Perhaps it wasn't such a good idea. He wasn't fit, not like he used to be.

Should he stay in the village, have lunch at the Gasthaus, and then wend his way down to the train station, back to Lucerne? He had made his pilgrimage, had said his prayers at his parents' grave, and seen his childhood home. What else was there to do?

The path to Obsee was just about visible. It snaked up through rocks and conifers vanishing into the gorge. It beckoned him. He had to go. The alp, after all, was his responsibility. When he was a boy, it had taken him two hours there and back; now it would take him longer.

Resolutely, Paul pulled his anorak from his knapsack. A sealed brown envelope fell to his feet. Wincing, he stuffed it back, retrieved his walking stick and set off.

He made good progress. 'There's still life in the old dog,' Paul said aloud and shook his fist at some unseen enemy. 'See if I can't outrun you, you bastard.'

The air in the gorge smelled musty and damp. Deep below, the Melchibach wound its way through boulders and uprooted trees. Paul shuddered and zipped up his anorak. The bleached trunks reminded him of prehistoric animal bones. In the distance, the first rumble of thunder and the mournful sound of the church's Angelus bell could be heard.

Placing each foot carefully, using the stones as steps, he climbed the path, occasionally stopping to put his hands on his knees, gasping. Coming out of the gorge, he started crossing the field of scree, a vast expanse of shale. Here and there, water sprung from deep fissures, making the surface treacherous. The sharp whistle of marmots sounded from between the boulders. Two golden eagles swooped along the overhanging edges of the cliffs, looking for prey.

He sat down, out of the keen wind, against a warm rock. Every so often, the sun's rays managed to break through the thickening cloud, lighting up the copper dome of the church and the village roofs far below him. Heavy shadows floated across the slopes opposite.

When he woke from a heavy slumber, he no longer saw blue sky but dark clouds obliterating the mountains. Lightning tore across the sky in quick succession.

It had taken him too long to come up here. He would have to stay the night - not to worry. His passage on the Nieuw Amsterdam, back to New York was not until the following week. He had mentioned to the hotel receptionist in Lucerne that he might be staying away a night or two.

He swallowed hard and wiped the back of his hands across his eyes when he stepped out of the larch copse. He and his family had always spent the summers up here. Although the land on this plateau was fertile, his father had never been one for

experiments. When Paul got older, he had wanted
to do his own thing, for the alp would be his one day:
extend the hut into a farmhouse and grow crops.
His father had just shaken his head and pointed his
finger at his forehead. The two had argued violently,
and Paul realised there was no room for both of
them. That's why he had left for the plains of
Canada.

With a farmer's pride, he watched the herd
of cows walking past. He had heard the tinkling of
their bells from afar. A drover's trail, clearly visible,
led up to the pass.

At the threshold to the hut, a large brindle
dog rose barking, baring his teeth.

'Quiet Barry!' A gruff voice came from the
shadows of the overhanging roof. 'God be with you,
Grüezi.'

Paul replied with the same greeting and
added, 'a bed in the hay for a weary traveller?'

The man nodded and pushed open the door. 'Yes, come in, the storm's going to break any minute.' As if to confirm this, a flash of lightning tore open the sky followed by a thunderclap.

'Get dry by the fire.' He took Paul's elbow and steered him towards the roaring fire in the grate.

A mop of white hair and a grey beard framed the man's weathered face. He wore the traditional embroidered smock of the alpine farmer.

Sitting by the open fireplace in rickety easy chairs, they didn't talk much. Exchanging pleasantries had never been easy for Paul. He was happy about the silence, which was occasionally interrupted by heavy thunderclaps shaking the hut. It was dark now, but the light created by the blazing logs lit up the heavily beamed interior of the cabin, one large room serving as sitting and kitchen area with a roughly hewn table and a corner bench. The door to the Stübli stood open, and Paul could see

the built-in bed covered by a gingham eiderdown
and pillows. A ladder led up to the hayloft,
extending the whole length of the hut and adjacent
stable.

Heavy rain tore at the windows and hit the
shingle roof. Shutters drummed against the wooden
boards. The wind roared through the fir trees
behind the cabin.

Once the storm had calmed, they sat at the table,
eating a simple meal of cheese, bread, and dried
meat.

'You're one of the Imholz lot, Päuli?' The
farmer pointed a callous hand at Paul.

'Yes, and you're Uli. Rohrer Uli. I reckon we
went to school together.'

Uli grimaced. 'Yes, and had a few
adventures.'

Paul nodded. They had got on well together, had a few rough and tumbles and several narrow escapes from his father's belt and Sister Dolores's ruler.

'You own this Alp.' Uli tapped the table and looked around him. 'I pays my dues come Martin's day, hope your brother has…'

Paul interrupted him. 'Yes, no worries, he puts the rent in my bank account.' His eyes swept around the room, taking in the new window frames and the fireplace. 'And you've taken good care of it.'

Uli coughed violently and wiped his mouth with the back of his sleeve. 'It will be my last summer up here. It's getting too much, not sure I can manage this season.' He pointed his pipe to the beam above them, at the numbers carved into the wood. 'My time on this earth is numbered.'

Paul nodded. With him, it had been arthritis first, and then that new pain, that nagging feeling of something more serious. He would open the letter tonight and decide what to do.

Later, in the hayloft, lying on a coarse linen sheet spread across the straw, Paul tore open the envelope and read it with the help of the torch he had borrowed. The news was what he expected; not entirely conclusive. He would try not to lose any sleep over it.

In the night rain slammed into the roof, and the wind tore at the shutters. The beams around him strained and moaned, the straw whispered.

He was a boy once more. His father called the Betruf through a wooden funnel, the prayer chant of the farmers, as the last rays of the sun set the mountains on fire and the evening wind stirred the grass and rippled the water of the lake. Soon other mountain farmers joined him from neighbouring alps, either chanting or blowing the Alphorns.

His mother made cheese, the cauldron hanging over the blazing logs, the sleeves of her simple grey dress turned up, a scarf holding back her chestnut hair.

Father worked in all weathers, cutting grass, building dry stonewalls, and repairing the hut.

In the evening, they sat on the bench under the overhanging roof and Mother went over the alphabet with them. He and his brother yodelled while milking the cows.

When it rained, they whittled wood at the kitchen table or did their sums while Mother kneaded the bread dough or knitted and darned their socks and jumpers. When the weather was good, they climbed the cliffs to prove how brave they were or swam across the ice-cold lake.

There were also sad times. He thought about his little sister. She died of measles before she was one. Her little waxen body was laid out in a roughly hewn coffin before they carried her down to the valley to be buried.

'God gives and God takes.' Paul could still hear his mother's sad but brave voice.

He woke to sun streaming through the roof light, playing with hundreds of dust motes. He pushed it open and before him spread the alpine pasture; this was his kingdom he had left and neglected for years. The mountains, like white paper cutouts, towered into a deep blue sky. The lake stood silent, glistening in the early morning sun. The cows grazed, following the age-old tracks winding up the slopes, washed by last night's rain.

Millions of years had come and gone. More tests were needed, the letter had confirmed.

However, he would put it on hold; there was work to be done. The dreams dreamt as a young man could now become a reality. He had enough money but perhaps not enough time.

He climbed down into the hut, savouring the smell of roasted coffee and freshly baked bread. Uli, Paul knew, had been up early, tending to the cows and starting on the cheese, milk boiling in the cauldron slung over the blazing logs.

Paul cleared his throat and joined Uli. 'I stay, I'll help you, together we'll manage.' He went over to the fire, threw the letter into the flames, and looked at Uli who prodded his pipe, clenched it between his teeth and nodded.

## The Visitors

Sammy punched the air. 'There. That's where we're heading.' He pointed to the farmhouse at the far side of the lake, smoke swirling from its chimney.

Behind the house, slopes of grass rose towards sheer cliffs, to the mountains capped with snow. A narrow trail wound its way between the boulders up to the pass.

Lisa scowled. 'Thanks for dragging our butts up here. First, you try to kill us by climbing this goat track, and now you expect us to stay up here in the middle of nowhere.' She poked Sammy in the back. 'Your plan kind of freaks me out. What if he recognises you? What then?'

Ziva, hands on her knees, gasped, 'Yes, Lisa's right. You're fucking scary; we can't just-'

'Don't worry,' Sammy interrupted Ziva and turned to face her. Lisa recoiled at the sight of him.

He looked deadly white - a good impression of a vampire, without the fangs. Lisa worried about his health, the cough that wracked his body every night.

'He won't know me, hasn't seen me since I was a small kid. We have no choice, need to keep our heads down for a while. Right?'

'I've had it up to here with this shit.' Lisa put the flat of her hand under her nose. A keen wind made her shiver.

Skirting the edge of the deep blue lake, Sammy kicked stones into the water while plodding on. Waves rippled across the pebbled foreshore. Tall and spindly, he strode ahead. His long black hair hung over the upturned collar of his coat, flapping like the wings of a mystical bird.

Lisa and Ziva ran after him. 'Hey, big guy,' Lisa called out. 'It was fun, stealing that Mercedes. You were good, in and out of all that traffic, and the speed. Wow!'

Sammy put his hands over his ears.

Ziva flapped her arms. 'Ha, yes, and pushing it down the ravine was best. I'll never forget that, hey, all that metal in a heap at the bottom.'

Lisa watched Ziva, feeling sorry for her. Every so often she staggered as if drunk but always righted herself quickly, not wanting to show any sign of weakness despite her anorexia. She was a terrific friend, always eager to please, fetching and carrying for Sammy and her. They both dressed like twins: short tartan skirts, biker jackets, and boots without laces. Their jet-black hair showed lines of re-growth.

Imholz Leo leaned against the doorframe and shielded his rheumy eyes. He had been watching the three ramblers approach.

Catching hold of his walking stick, he limped into the yard. Although he didn't mind the solitude, it would be nice to talk to someone.

Leo looked up at his farmhouse and thought back to his cousin, Paul, who after the war had returned from Canada and had extended a simple alpine hut into this comfortable dwelling. That same year, the forestry commission had extended the road from Untersee. Paul had lived up here for a few years, happy and content. The growing of various crops was a success, and he had been rightfully proud. Leo got on well with him, and his sudden death came as a shock to everyone. First, Paul's boys rented out the farm to a couple who ran it as a Gasthof but later Leo was offered to buy it for a song.

His daughter seldom visited, and when she did, she kept on about putting the farm in her name. Sure as anything, she was up to some jiggery-pokery. However, he would have the last word. Leo smiled and tapped the side of his nose.

It was getting late. The sun had sunk behind the mountains, leaving red and purple streaks in the sky.

The three walkers started to run towards the hut, hollering and screaming arms outstretched. Leo nodded. They were teenagers, wearing completely unsuitable clothes for rambling. Whenever he could get hold of a newspaper, he would read it, religiously, from front to back. These young people were Punks or Goths perhaps?

The young man was the ringleader. Through clenched teeth, he said, 'We have to stay here for a while,' and marched to the front door and beckoned the girls to follow.

When Leo caught up with them, they were slumped on the corner bench around the kitchen table. It was evident that the young man was not well. He clutched his face as if in agony, a child's face with the first shadow of a moustache. Somehow, he looked familiar. But no, he'd never met these kids before. They were probably from Lucerne. What did they want? To stay for a while, the boy had said.  Why? Why would they want to stay with an old man and a few cows, in the middle of nowhere? Surely, they had been up to no good. Leo shrugged his shoulders. He was used to sheltering walkers when the weather turned bad; he would cope with these hooligans. A gust of wind shook the window frame and caught in the chimney, making the embers in the range crackle and hiss.

One of the girls put her feet on the table. 'Have you got any drink? I mean not bloody coffee, but like Schnaps or Beer.'

Leo winced. How rude these youngsters were! No need to worry; they were nothing but grumpy children. He understood. Youngsters didn't have it easy nowadays.

Leo had been lucky. Married to his Mathilda, God rest her soul, they had been blissfully happy up here. Today, young people couldn't even dream of buying their own home. At least he would see his grandson right. Samuel had not visited him for years, but he'd written over the farm to him. If he didn't want to live here, he could rent it out or sell it. It would fetch a pretty penny.

'I'm Imholz Leo. What are your names?' Leo asked, sitting on his three-legged stool near the fire, stuffing his pipe.

'No need to know.' The young man shivered. Leo got up, took a blanket from the bench and draped it around the boy's shoulders. The lad looked at him with deep blue eyes. Eyes he had seen before, vulnerable and childlike.

'Is there any grub for my mates?' The girl who looked like a skeleton stood on tiptoes, searching the built-in dresser. She pulled out a packet of biscuits and a piece of cheese and flung it on the table. They found the Schnapps Leo had legally distilled for his cows to ease their calving.

Passing one of the bottles round, they each took swigs from it, coughing and spluttering.

'What's it with those weird numbers on the beam in the hallway? I noticed when we came in, looks spooky,' the young man said, his teeth chattering. Was he trying to make conversation? Perhaps he felt sorry for the girls' behaviour.

Leo didn't know. The boy was right; he'd always found them eerie too. He had intended to plane them out.

Later, the young people bedded down upstairs, in one of the spare rooms. Leo went to sleep in his easy chair next to the kitchen range.

In the night, he heard the boy cough, wheeze and soft voices trying to calm him. He wondered what was wrong with the lad. No doubt, they had been sleeping rough, catching colds or worse.

Voices woke Leo. He limped to the door. Two climbers, carrying heavy backpacks, wished him good morning and vanished towards the pass. Should he have said something? Maybe he should have asked them to alert the police. His visitors might be dangerous. No, he would go and milk the few cows he had left and then prepare breakfast for his visitors.

On the way back from the barn, Leo leant against the house wall, his heart beating fast. A sea of pain took hold of his chest, squeezed and released it, only to squeeze even tighter. Slowly he slid down onto the paving stones, sitting there for a while, catching his breath. Fits like this happened more and more often but were always short-lived. He laboured into a standing position, let himself back into the house and shuffled along the hall. He pulled himself up the banister to the first floor. The youngsters nestled together, fast asleep on the large bed. The three looked like children: one of the girls sucked her thumb; the other twisted a strand of hair.

The boy lay curled up. At last, he had found some rest.

Lisa woke first. The smell of toasted bread and coffee had drifted into the bedroom. She sniffed the air with a smile. A child once more she snuggled under her soft duvet, listening to her mum moving around in the kitchen. Lisa was knackered. She had it up to wherever with their sort of life, staying in squats. Now, after their latest prank, they would no doubt be involved with the law. The filth was bound to catch up with them. She wanted to go home; she wanted her mum.

Lisa admired the old man. He was strong all right, not showing that he was pissed off with them last night. He'd just been patient, kind and hadn't lost his cool. How come?

She crept down to the kitchen, keen to talk to Leo before the others woke to reassure him that they meant no harm. Yes, Sammy was a grumpy git but had a good heart. His so-called father fucking off to America and his mother on the bottle had made him bitter and angry. And there was something else Lisa wanted to tell Leo: she knew from her nan that this was important to the older generation, Sammy never swore. He was not like her and Ziva; he was much more posh. He never foul-mouthed everything like they did.

'What the hell...?' In the semi darkness of the kitchen, she had stepped on something soft.

Leo had slumped against the table and just lay there his eyes open, staring blindly at the ceiling. She felt for a pulse. There was none.

Lisa pulled herself up and tore at her hair. Her eyes wide, her mouth contorted, she screamed.

Ziva and Sammy came running down the stairs. They stared down at the body and then at the table with breakfast ready, toasted bread, slices of cheese and dried meat, jam, and the coffee pot ready to pour. It seemed as though Leo was just about to call them.

Tears streaked Lisa's cheeks. Ziva clasped her face in her hands.

Samuel fell on his knees and cradled Leo in his arms. He put his face against his grandfather's cheeks and sobbed.

## Snowfall

Untersee, Christmas 1993

My dear Charles,

I have made my decision and therefore hasten to take up my pen, fulfilling an old promise to you, my dear friend, relating the events of that fateful Christmas of 1959, which made me what I am.

For many years, I have rarely gone out; I have spent the long days walking up and down my study in a threadbare dressing gown and writing. Yes, that muse has been my companion.

As my English publisher, you know that I have written numerous books but why could I never put in words what happened when I was a boy? I tried many a time but it was always a game of hide and seek. They were there, the memories, hiding in the grey matter of my brain. Why could I never catch them? Every so often, even beyond her grave, I hear my mother's nagging but anxious voice. 'Be careful what you write, Son!'

I invite you to travel with me to Obsee, in the Swiss Mountains.

I was twelve when Father decided that we would spend Christmas in Obsee. In despair, I had rested my head on my arms. I groaned. This place in the mountains was at the end of the world. Just one thing spoke for it: the train journey from Zürich on the SBB. Mother made soothing noises and Father peered over the rim of his spectacles and told her to be quiet.

Obsee was familiar to me from our last summer vacations: mountains that set your teeth on edge for they resembled the jagged fangs of primeval animals. The waterlogged cliffs were too slippery to climb and the lake, at whose muddy shore the house sat, was too cold to swim. Herds of cows, wearing bells, grazed aimlessly.

Gasthof Obsee was a small hostelry. Herr and Frau Trun, the tenants, took in a few paying guests.

It still makes me shiver when I think back to that evening when we arrived in the village square of Untersee on the last post bus, in icy fog.

Our landlord materialised out of a soupy fog. His hump was hidden by a blanket pulled over his shoulder. He loaded our luggage on the motorised sled and my parents climbed into the seat next to him. I crouched with our bags on the dickey seat. Clutching the steering wheel like the horns of a wild animal, he drove off in a cloud of snow.

Mother tried to grasp Father's arm, but he shook her off.

Coming above the fog line, the mountains were no longer rotten teeth but sugar cones, twinkling in the evening sun. Slopes of white led down to the lake, frozen into a sheet of ice.

The traditional Swiss house with an overhanging roof and shuttered windows, stood stark against the snow-covered slopes. A bank of grey clouds, tinged with yellow, had crept in from the west and had swallowed the mountains - a sure sign of more snow. We might be marooned for weeks.

The walls and ceilings throughout the house were panelled in knotty wood. Simple gingham curtains adorned the windows and the furniture was of traditional pine, roughly hewn. In the lounge, a fire blazed and the flickering of the flames projected dancing shadows on the walls.

'Das Nachtessen ist genau um sechs,' Frau Trun said briskly. Nobody dared to appear late for any meal, for our hosts were formidable. She was large as a house and he was as thin as a willow. She was slow and languid and he was quick of foot and temper. Once I had seen a meat cleaver fly across the kitchen, landing in the doorjamb.

I always occupied the same tiny attic room, while my parents had one of the first floor rooms complete with Kachelofen.

The only other guest in the dining room that evening was a woman of uncertain age. Her hair was a mass of ginger ringlets, her skin white as snow, and she looked at me with dark big eyes. Or was it my father she was staring at? I used my serviette to hide my face, dabbing my mouth after each bite of fried fish and steamed potatoes served by Herr Trun who had exchanged his blanket for a white waiter's jacket. Only when eating my favourite dessert - chocolate mousse - was I able to forget her liquid gaze.

Father introduced us. 'Herr and Frau Baumann and Herbert, my son. We hail from Zürich.' In Switzerland, nobody uses first names unless you happen to be a child. Therefore, it was Herbert for me, a name I hated. I quite often introduced myself as Clark, Clark Gable. That sounded so much more impressive.

Her name was Frau Krähenfuss. She was German, from Frankfurt.

I pressed my napkin to my face and sniggered. What a name! Crow's feet!

Father prodded me in the side. Never taking his eyes off her, he asked, 'You are alone?'

She nodded. 'Yes, just for tonight.' The emphasis was on tonight. 'My husband is arriving tomorrow with two friends, interesting people.' She turned and fastened her eyes on me again. 'And a little friend for you, Herbert.'

'What?' I exclaimed in horror and swallowed empty. That was the last thing I needed, a little brat bothering me.

'You are not pleased, young whippersnapper?' Her face came so close I could see her spidery lashes, her crow's feet and red flecks in her eyes.

She cackled. 'I didn't realise the horserace was today.'

I knew straight away that she was referring to my buckteeth. Throwing the napkin on the table, I clenched my fists.

Father roared with laughter, and Mother put her arm around me. I put my head against her chest and felt her heart beat wildly. Pulling myself free, I ran up to my room and threw myself on the bed.

I couldn't sleep, so at midnight I got up, stood on tiptoes, and raised the roof light. An ethereal fog, made up of thousands of tiny stars, whirled round and round. It was snowing.

Although I had always been a rather cowardly boy I took the torch, descended the rickety stairs and knocked on my parents' room. There was no answer. The door was locked. I saw a streak of light across the floor of the hall. Crowfeet's room. I gently turned the knob and the door opened, just a crack.

My father was a fast worker, be it with our frequently changing maids or any female acquaintances. Moreover, he had locked my mother into their room. How dare he? I banged my head against the doorjamb synchronising it with the creaking of the bed.

In the morning, the snowstorm had abated and I climbed down from my attic room and joined my parents at breakfast. Father poured coffee while mother buttered slices of bread. 'Happy Christmas Eve,' my mother said, patting my arm. I nestled against her.

'Did you sleep well, child?' Father asked. I detested him calling me child.

Crowfeet's face looked naked, not made up like last night. She moaned, 'Frau Trun just told me that the road down to Untersee is impassable, too much snow.' She wiped her eyes with a serviette. 'I always said it: this is a godforsaken place. We are cut off. My husband and friends will have to spend the festivities down in the village.' I breathed a sigh of relief, no kid to spoil my Christmas.

Glancing sideways at my father, I saw a glint in his eyes, not the 'dirty old man' glint, no, this time it was a 'knight to the rescue' kind of look.

'No problem, a little bit of snow won't stop us. Herr Trun will let me use his motorised sledge! We'll fetch them from the post auto.' Father stopped short of making a boy scout salute.

Crowfeet laid her manicured claws on my father's hand. 'Wonderful; they'll arrive at Untersee mid-afternoon.'

After breakfast, I went outside. Thick clouds hid the mountains. Herr Trun beckoned me; his hands curled like the talons of a bird, 'Hallo! Herbert, komm, hilf mir mit dem Weihnachtsbaum.' Yes, I was pleased to be asked and always willing to help.

Herr Trun pushed the sled from the shed. We drove off; the plough sweeping the snow into walls either side. At the pine copse, we stopped and our landlord limped to one of the firs and swung his axe. I ran my hands over the steering wheel of the snow vehicle. In those days, I was fascinated by anything mechanical. This contraption was cobbled together from an old convertible, the front wheels immobilised by the sledge-runners. I knelt down, looked underneath and nodded.

During lunch Crowfeet and Father flirted, while Mother looked on, eyes damp and lips pressed together. Every so often, she wrung her hands. She held onto my arm and squeezed it.

Lunch over, Crowfeet fetched her furs. The fox's head hanging down her back grinned at me. She pressed against Father who waited for her in the vehicle. He drove a trial run around the Gasthof and they vanished in a cloud of snow.

Small avalanches of snow cascaded down the steep slope.

The sled raced away, skimming the side of the mountain, the tops of poles indicating where the track was. At a steep bend, the vehicle performed a few slalom movements. The stretch of road they were on had probably been cleared by the forestry commission and had iced up. The rev of the engine echoed around the cliffs. Father tried to get up to the bank to halt the contraption, but instead picked up speed, ever more. And then... I didn't trust my eyes. Through a haze of crazed delight, I spotted motor, furs and bodies flying through the air into the black mouth of the gorge. I turned round and saw Mother hovering behind me. She frowned. Slowly her face relaxed and her tight lips widened into a smile, which she quickly suppressed.

Dear Charles, you have always admonished me for hurrying the end of my jottings, but I find it hard to elaborate any further. I think you can rhyme things together.

As soon as it got dark, the candles on the Christmas trees were lit. The host passed around Glühwein and cookies and wondered why Father and Krähenfuss had not returned yet with the party of guests. The phone call came through that the mountain rescue had found two bodies in the gorge.

After the tragic event, Mother took me back to Zurich and engaged a private tutor, not letting me out of her sight. Since her death, I have lived the life of a recluse.

Prisons come in various guises.

Every year I make a pilgrimage back to Untersee. The Gasthof Obsee is no longer. Herr und Frau Trun retired shortly after the incident.

I am staying at the local inn.

This will be my last trip. Everything is in hand. You will be instructed by my solicitors.

I look up from my writing. The mountains loom above me. They resemble two faces, staring down at me in perpetual condemnation. They beckon me!

I remain yours faithfully,

Herbert

## Christmas Harvest

Johan stood against the door of his farmstead, staring out over the valley below. He had observed the black spot in the snowy landscape for some time. Gradually it had assumed the form of a man labouring through deep snow. The solitary figure struggled over the brow of the hill and onto the plateau. In his right hand, he gripped a solid wooden stick; in the other, he clutched a large envelope. Every so often, he slipped in the frozen snow, swore, righted himself and carried on. He was dressed in hunting green, and his bowed legs formed a perfect O.

The sky was overcast. Deep hanging clouds had swallowed the mountains, and it was getting dark.

When the mayor of Untersee saw Johan standing in the doorway, he touched the brim of his hat as if to salute, and Johan bowed his head in exaggerated subservience.

'I watched ye for a while, mayor. It must be bad tidings ye bring, coming up in person.'

The mayor cleared his throat. 'Ay, it's not good, Johan. Not news ye want to hear, a few weeks before Christmas.' He handed him the envelope. 'This would be yer notice for the lease of this house and the land.' He stood back and waved his hand encompassing all: the heavily beamed wooden house with its low overhanging roof, the shuttered windows letting through streaks of light, the adjoining stable, and the meadows now under a thick eiderdown of snow. 'I'm sorry, to be sure, and this so near Christmas.'

Johan stood there, the envelope in his hand, looking at it from under bushy eyebrows, twisting it this way and that. 'A month's notice for the lease of this house?' he said. 'Ye mean they want us out?'

'Ay, your landlord, Samuel Imholz, has sold the house. The young whippersnapper. Wants the money no doubt.' The major rubbed his thumb and finger together and carried on. 'Well, it is as it is! Apparently, the new owner is a proper fine gentleman from town. He's going to renovate the house and wants to come here with his family to recuperate.' The mayor lifted his hat and made a sweeping gesture. 'I've got to go; had my exercise for today. It's getting dark; all the details are in the letter.' He pointed his chin at the envelope.

Johan's heart was heavy when he crossed the hallway. He squinted up at the beam with the carved numbers. That's how long they would be able to stay here, a month, 30 days. He would be homeless soon, homeless with his wife and five young children. He placed the envelope on the kitchen table and brushed his hand on his twill trousers as if the very paper were contagious.

That evening, his wife Grete wrote a few lines on Johan's behalf. The soft glow of the first Advent candle formed a halo around her auburn hair. She clenched the fountain pen in work-worn hands, carefully forming letters.

Dear Sir from town,

Please can we stay in our house, we cannot find shelter anywhere that quickly.

God bless,

Johan

On Christmas Eve, the postman, on his moped, slipped and slid through the snow, delivering a letter from the gentlemen in town.

Johan groaned, but his eyes smiled, 'We can stay for one more harvest. But as soon as that harvest is safely under cover, we've got to get out.'

'One more harvest,' moaned Grete. 'One more harvest,' echoed the children when they had finished singing 'Silent Night' under the Christmas tree. Johan's gaze wandered around the room - he looked, he blinked, and he cheered up - to stay for just one more harvest wasn't as bad as all that.

When the villagers from Untersee saw Johan walking through the alleyways of the village whistling and downing a pint in the Gasthof, they were surprised how unconcerned Johan seemed.

'Don't ye want to start looking for another farm to lease, ye know how quickly time goes.' They turned their hats and kicked their hobnail boots against the floorboards. 'A few months and the harvest is in, and ye have to move out.'

With good humour, Johan slapped their shoulders and tapped the side of his nose. 'Well, why so much in a hurry? I'm sure something will show itself.'

Johan spread muck on top of the snowy fields. All the goodness of the manure filtered down into the soil he had ploughed in the autumn.

Spring arrived, and with it came the big thaw. The snow melted from the rooftop dripping from the wooden guttering. It melted from the fields and revealed fertile, rich soil. The first buds appeared on the trees. The snowdrops drilled their sharp buds up through the hard earth and the short green grass.

Johan drove his ancient tractor down to the neighbouring market town and bargained with the seed merchant. With several hessian sacks on his flatbed wagon, he returned through the village, at breakneck speed.

From then on, he was busy from morning until night; for he put in the seeds by hand, one after the other, neatly three inches apart and one inch deep. It took him a long time to do his planting.

Every day Johan was in his fields hoeing. Not one single weed was allowed its existence. Using the water from the small lake, he set up an ingenious irrigation system with old hose pipes which he begged and borrowed but not stole, not Johan.

In June, some of the farmers from Untersee came huffing and puffing up to the Obsee and inspected the fields. They walked up and down and hither and thither but could not find one single green shoot. Nothing was showing.

They told the folk in the village the bad news, 'Nothing's growing; we reckon his seeds have died. He won't even have one harvest.'
In August they came back, huffing and puffing, and found that tiny little shoots had appeared through the soil, but they were so teeny weeny, it amounted to nothing.

A beautiful summer went into an even more splendid autumn.

The November storms came and with them the rich gentleman from town. He drove his expensive car up the winding mountain road. Gravel hit the side of the shiny chassis, making it sound like gunfire. His wife clutched her seat, her knuckles white, her face distorted. He parked halfway up the slope, and the couple trudged the rest of the way, over the brow of the hill, onto the plateau. The woman was wrapped in an ermine coat, her hair perfectly coiffed.

The seedlings, now the size of a hand's width, made them shake their heads. The man scratched his beard, cleaned his glasses and shrugged his shoulders. The woman toppled, bent down and retrieved a broken-off stiletto heel, holding it like a weapon. When she spotted the farmhouse in the distance, a shiver went down her spine. She dug her manicured long nails into her husband's arm and hissed, 'Is that it? You want me to come on holiday here?'

Christmas came and went. The seedlings were buried under a deep blanket of snow. Every so often, Johan went out on to his fields, dug a hole in the snow and looked at his crop tenderly.

To keep their heads above water, Johan went to work in the sawmill in the valley and Grete worked in the Gasthof in Untersee.

In early Spring, Johan hitched the muck spreader to the tractor, and with his youngest son on his lap sprayed the snow with manure from his cows and pigs. The child squealed with delight when the brown liquid painted patterns on the white canvas. The wind and weather did their jobs, the snow thawed; it froze into jagged crystals and melted again. Eventually the manure filtered slowly into the dark earth below, nourishing the seedlings.

Spring arrived, and the melting snow revealed plants strong and healthy, ready for inspection. The villagers trooped up to Johan's fields and saw swathes of green, each plant a perfect little pyramid. The burghers squinted, rubbed their noses and hitched their shoulders up to their ears.

When they asked Johan as to the nature of his crops, he just tapped his nose. Grete, who every Sunday went down to the village to attend church, saw all the ladies crowd around her. She just shook her head, tied her scarf tighter over her auburn hair and climbed back up to their homestead without uttering a word. The seed merchant didn't spill the beans either.

Advent came, and Johan and his family looked forward to their second Christmas of reprieve. They weren't surprised when a letter came from the gentleman in town saying his patience was sorely tested, and that he wasn't prepared to wait forever.

Again, Johan told Grete to write a letter.

Dear Sir in town,
I am sorry that the harvest is so long coming and that ye can't take over the farmstead sooner. But it will take some more time. Before it started to snow, I transplanted and thinned the seedlings grown from seeds sown two years ago. I now have over a thousand healthy plants. Our Christmas trees will be harvested in six years or thereabouts. I am truly sorry about it taking so long, but would ye give me

some more time and wishing a happy Christmas to
all.
Gratefully,
Johan

They didn't hear back for four long weeks.
Then on Christmas Eve, at last, the postman, on his
moped, brought an answer from the gentleman in
town.

Johan stared down at the letter, swallowed
empty, pulled himself up, tugged at his braces and
started to dance a jig. 'He says..., he says..., we can
stay, he understands.' He took hold of Grete and
swung her round and round. The children clung to
their legs and danced with them.

When Johan regained his breath, he carried
on, 'Just listen to that. The gentleman's bought a
villa in warmer climes. They no longer want a house
out in the sticks, where they'd be snowed in every
winter. We can stay as long as we want.'

The whole family added another turn to their
jig, while under the deep snow a thousand tiny

Christmas trees waited patiently for future
Christmases to come.

# Das Haus in den Bergen

Diese Kurzgeschichten-Sammlung sind
Erzählungen aus den Schweizer Bergen. Alles spielt
sich in derselben Gegend, im gleichen Haus ab. Die
Geschichten kann man unabhänging voneinander
lesen.

Diese Erzählungen widme ich meinem Mami das in den Bergen wohnte und gern Kurzgeschichten las. Sie hätte sie auch in Englisch gelesen, da sie mit achtzig immer noch eifrig Englisch lernte.

Ich bin Maren, Vera und meiner Schwester Antonia dankbar für die Korrekturen

Mit herzlichem Dank auch an meine Lieblingsschriftsteller und Vorbilder: Thomas Hardy, Amelia B. Edwards, Susan Hill, Jeremias Gotthelf, Thomas Mann und viele mehr.

# DAS HAUS IN DEN BERGEN

## Die Rückkehr

Anna schob die Riemen des schweren Tragkorbes zurecht. Sie öffnete ihren Mantel und lockerte den steifen Kragen ihrer Bluse. Der Rock klebte an den gestrickten Strümpfen. Eine Haarsträhne hing ihr ins Gesicht und sie steckte diese ungeduldig in ihren Knoten zurück.

Über Alpenwiesen schlängelte sich der Pfad hinauf zum kleinen Dorf Untersee.

„Napoleon", rief sie leise, „Fuss! Guter Hund." Sie umklammerte seine Halsmähne und eilte an den verwitterten Bauernhäusern und der weissgetünchten Kapelle vorbei. Sie wollte niemandem begegnen. Man würde sich wundern was sie so spät im Herbst auf der Alp verloren hatte.

Als sie das letzte Haus des Dorfes hinter sich gelassen hatte, hörte sie eine Stimme. „Anna, wart!"

Sie stand stockstill, seufzte und hob die Augen zum Himmel. Hans! Als Kinder hatten sie zusammen die Schulbank im Pfarrhaus gedrückt. Jetzt sahen sie sich in der Kirche oder auf dem Markt und hie und da plauderten sie zusammen.

Hans umklammerte ihren Arm. „Potz! Du gehst auf die Alp. So spät im Herbst?"

„He jo. Mein Vater und ich brachten das Vieh ins Tal hinunter und nun gehe ich zurück und warte dort auf meinen Mann. Von dort ging er fort und dorthin wird er zurückkommen."

Hans streifte die Lederriemen des Tragkorbes von ihren Achseln und nahm ihr die schwere Last von den Schultern.

„Ich trag dir die Hutte." Er schob seine Arme in die Riemen und schulterte den Korb. „Hab im Moment nichts besseres zu tun."

Anna zuckte hilflos die Schultern. „Mir a! Wenn d'wotsch."

Mit seinen genagelten Schuhen trat Hans einen
Stein aus dem Weg. „Ich will dir nicht Angst
machen aber die Nachrichten aus der Lombardei
sind schlecht. Hätten Peter oder seine Kameraden
überlebt, wären sie schon lange zurück...", er
unterbrach sich und hustete.

Anna stolperte. Sie versuchte sich aufrecht zu
halten, tapfer zu sein. Was wusste Hans schon?
Peter lebte. Er hatte ihr versprochen, noch bevor es
einwinterte wieder daheim zu sein.

Sie kraulte Napoleon's Fell und schluckte den Kloss
im Hals hinunter. Sie hatte den Hund von Peter
bekommen als er als Söldner in fremde
Kriegsdienste zog. Sie hatten ihm den Namen
Napoleon gegeben, ein zutreffender Name, ihr
Mann kämpfte schliesslich in der Armee des
berühmten Feldherrn. Peter würde von dieser
seiner letzten Kampagne als reicher Mann
zurückkommen. Dann konnten sie sich einen
kleinen Bauernhof im Flachland leisten. Hier oben

brachte man es zu nichts. Ihr Vater hatte während Jahren für wenig geschuftet.

In der Schlucht konnte man den Himmel kaum sehen. Felsen türmten sich auf beiden Seiten. Die kühle Feuchtigkeit und das Tosen des Baches gaben ihr Gänsehaut. Es roch nach Moos und vermodertem Holz. Ausgelaugte Baumstämme erinnerten sie an Tierskelette.

Napoleon,  gross wie ein Kalb, lief voraus, rannte aber immer wieder zurück um sich zu vergewissern, dass sie ihm auch wirklich folgte.


Der Pfad wand sich steil über Stoppelfelder und ganz oben verschwand er zwischen Felsen. Von dort wollte sie allein das Geröllfeld überqueren. Sie wollte nicht, dass Hans mit ihr auf die Alp kam. Nach dem ersten Herbststurm war die Hütte in schlechtem Zustand. Er würde aufs Dach klettern um die heruntergefallenen Ziegel zu ersetzen, würde sich an den Fensterläden, die von rostigen

Angeln hingen, zu schaffen machen und sich ereifern, dass es nichts sei für eine Frau im Winter dort oben allein zu hausen.

Bei einem Felsbrocken blieben sie stehen und mit den Händen auf die Knie gestützt, verschnauften sie.

„Gang jetzt! Du musst nicht mitkommen, in einer halben Stunde bin ich oben." Anna zog am Tragkorb.

„He, nur mit der Ruhe." Hans versuchte die Last neu zu schultern aber Anna hatte die Riemen schon in der Hand und zog ihn in die Hocke. Nach kurzem hin und her half er Anna schlussendlich die Last auf ihre Schultern zu heben.

Er beugte sich über sie, seine Hände auf ihren Hüften. „Du bist verrückt, weisst du überhaupt was es heisst einen ganzen Winter dort oben allein zu hausen?"

Ungeduldig entzog sich Anna.

„Mo mol, das weiss ich. Aber ich habe Milch von den Geissen, die mir Vater da gelassen hat, damit kann ich Käse machen! Im Kamin hängt geräuchertes Fleisch, und schau ich hab Mehl, Haferflocken und Zucker in der Hutte."

Sie zeigte über ihre Schultern in den Tragkorb und fügte bei, „und vergiss nicht, Peter kehrt zurück, das weiss ich. Dann kommen wir ins Tal hinunter bevor es einwintert." Trotzig verschränkte sie die Arme. „In der Zwischenzeit warte ich dort oben."

Sie setzte einen Fuss vor den andern, vorsichtig, jede Schieferplatte prüfend. Dann drehte sie sich um und rief, „danke dir, Hans, für das Tragen."

Hans hob seine Hand. „Uf Wiederluege! Ich komme dann mal vorbei wenn's auf die Jagd geht."

Anna zuckte zusammen und verzog das Gesicht. Sie wollte keine Besucher.

Jeden Schritt geplant, überquerte sie das Geröllfeld. Wasser quoll unter dem Schiefer hervor und es war schlüpfrig. Nur nicht hinunterschauen, nicht daran denken was passieren würde wenn sie hier ausrutschte und über den steilen Abhang in die Schlucht hinunterstürzte.

Als sie den letzten Hügel erklommen hatte, sah sie im Dämmerlicht die Alphütte vor sich. Sie klebte am steilen Hang, ein Blockhaus, mit angebautem Stall. Ueber dem Seeli stiegen Wiesen hinauf zu den Klippen.

Ein uralter Schmuggelpfad schlängelte sich zwischen Felsblöcken hinauf zum Pass. Über diesen Pass war Peter nach Italien gegangen und hier würde sie für ihn Ausschau halten, jeden Tag.

Vielleicht hatte Hans recht? Bald würde die Hütte unter tiefem Schnee begraben sein. Was wäre wenn Peter nicht zurückkäme, wenn sie vergebens, den ganzen Winter lang, auf ihn warten würde?

Anna war es sich gewohnt auf der Alp zu hausen. Frühmorgens molk sie die beiden Geissen. Dann füllte sie ihre Henkeltasse und Napoleons Napf mit

der schäumenden Milch und streute dem Hund
eine Handvoll Haferflocken hinein. Für seine
Abendmahlzeit jagte er sich einen Hasen oder frass
die Mäuse die er fing.

Sie hängte das Kessi über das Feuer um Wasser für
ihren Kaffee - ihr einziger Luxus - zu kochen. Sie
schnitt sich ein Stück Brot ab und strich den
selbstgemachten Weichkäse und Heidelbeerkonfi
drauf. Während sie den Hebel der Kaffeemühle
drehte summte sie ein Kirchenlied.

Einmal in der Woche leerte sie Milch ins Kessi und
machte Käse und buk Brot. Für ihren Mann. Sie
machte alles für ihn. Das würde sie ihm auftischen
wenn er endlich heimkam.

Die Sonne sank früh hinter den Firsten. Eine Kerze
und das Feuer im Kamin verbreiteten ein
heimeliges Licht. Sie setzte sich auf die Eckbank
und las die Bibel oder die Geschichte von Pestalozzi:
„Lienhard und Gertrud" die sie sicher schon
hundertmal gelesen hatte. Der Schluss gefiel ihr,

alles kam gut; genau so würde es für  Peter und sie sein.

Sie ging früh ins Bett, stieg die Leiter hinauf in den Heuboden wo sie auf einer Lage Stroh schlief. Ein Jutesack, vollgestopft mit Laub, hielt sie warm. Der Wind der um die Hütte heulte, flüsterte ihr Worte zu. Auch die Balken und Bodenbretter waren ihre Freunde; sie stöhnten und quietschten und erzählten ihr von früher. Vom Stall kam das Rascheln und Meckern der Geissen und lullten sie in den Schlaf.

Die Tage wurden kürzer. Eines Morgens versuchte Anna, die Fensterläden aufzustossen aber vergebens. Während der Nacht hatte es geschneit und ein Sturm hatte den Schnee gegen die Hütte geweht. Sie warf ein Scheit in die Feuerstelle, und heisse Asche flog in den Kamin. Das Feuer starb und sie war im Dunkeln. Sie fuhr zusammen. Was jetzt? Sie war in der Hütte eingeschlossen, gefangen. Aber dann fing das Holz wieder an zu glühen und die Flammen tauchten den Raum in ein goldenes Licht.

Sie machte sich an die Arbeit, grub sich wie ein Maulwurf aus der Hütte und befreite die Fenster von der Schneelast.

Peter war unentwegt in ihren Gedanken. Jede Nacht vor der Einschlafen sah sie ihn deutlich vor sich, wie er sich durch den hohen Schnee über den Pass kämpfte, zurück zu ihr. Nun da der Winter eingebrochen war, würden sie, hier oben, in trauter Gemeinsamkeit auf den Frühling warten.

Aber da war auch ein Albtraum der sie anfing zu plagen. Es war immer der gleiche: Mit gezücktem Bajonett kämpfte sich Peter inmitten einer Schar Soldaten Millimeter um Millimeter über ein blutiges Schlachtfeld vor. Mit ausgestreckten Händen versuchte sie ihn einzufangen, aber jedesmal entzog er sich ihr.

Schweissgebadet wachte sie dann auf und zitterte am ganzen Körper.

Eines Tages zog sie all ihre Kleider aus und nahm ein Bad im Schnee. Sie schaute an sich hinunter und zuckte zusammen. Sie war abgemagert, die Rippen standen hervor. Ihr Selbstvertrauen war verschwunden und sie fragte sich wie sie in dieser Einsamkeit weiter überleben konnte. Wegen des mageren Futters hatten die Geissen aufgehört Milch zu geben. Sie hatte nur noch ganz wenig Mehl und Haferflocken. War es ein oder zwei Monate her seit sie richtig gegessen hatte?

Vielleicht hatte Hans recht. Wenn Peter noch lebte, wäre er, bevor es einwinterte, zurückgekommen. Sie verschränkte die Arme und schüttelte sich.

„Nein, ich gebe nicht auf", schrie sie in den Wintermorgen hinein.

Anna hatte einen Kalender in einen der Holzbalken gekerbt. Mit einem verkohlten Stück Holz strich sie jeden Tag durch. Weihnachten war schon lange vorbei. Es war ungefähr Mitte März, aber der Frühling hier oben würde auf sich warten lassen.

Schneefälle zwangen Anna immer wieder in der Hütte zu bleiben. Aber wenn sie konnte lief sie hinaus und starrte auf den Pass, presste ihre Augen fest zusammen und sah Peter zwischen den Felsen und dem gefrorenen Wasserfall. Zuerst würde sie ihn als schwarzen Punkt in der Schneelandschaft erkennen; dann würde er immer näher kommen, der Mann den sie liebte. Nicht in Uniform aber in seinem alten Mantel mit zerbeultem Hut auf seinem Kopf, ein Tornister auf dem Rücken und ein Wanderstock in seiner Rechten. Der tiefe Schnee war ein Kinderspiel für ihn.

Eines Morgens als sie sich an der Feuerstelle wärmte, hörte sie ein Kratzen an der Tür und das ungeduldige Riegeln der Türfalle.

„Peter!" Annas Herz klopfte. Sie sprang vom Schemel und riss die Tür auf.

Sie zuckte entäuscht zusammen als sie Hans, der sich den Schnee von den Schuhen klopfte, auf der Schwelle sah.

„Was, nur du?"

Er hatte ein erlegtes Reh auf dem Rücken und warf es auf den Boden. Das Gewehr stellte er hinter die Tür.

Obwohl Anna zuerst entäuscht war, hüpfte sie bald geschäftig hin und her, mahlte den  Kaffee, den sie für Peter aufgespart hatte, warf ein Holzscheit in den Kamin und setzte das Kessi mit Wasser auf. Das Brot, das ihr Hans mitgebracht hatte, schnitt sie in dicke Scheiben. Ihr Besucher schaute schmunzelnd zu wie sie munter drauf los schnabulierte.

„Hesch rächt gha, es war nicht immer leicht hier oben, aber lueg, ich habe es trotzdem geschafft." Sie schaute Hans mit glänzenden Augen an. „He, was dänksch? Ich hatte keine Zeit zum Grübeln. Ha, und jedesmal wenn der Schnee die Hütte vergrub habe ich mich freigeschaufelt."

Hans nickte nur und liess sie reden.

„Peter kommt im Frühling, das weiss ich, habs geträumt." Sie stand vor Hans, die Schultern zurück, das Kinn vorgestreckt.

Die Lippen ihres Besuchers waren dünne Striche. Er sprang auf und ergriff ihre Schultern und schüttelte sie. „Mach dir doch nichts vor, der ist schon lange tot."

Anna starrte ihn an und strich sich über die Augen als ob sie Spinnengewebe entfernen wollte. So, das war es also, all das Warten auf ihren Mann war nichts als eine Totenwache gewesen.

Hans blieb den ganzen Tag, schnitt das Reh in Stücke und briet es über dem Feuer. Später kletterte sie mit ihm auf den Heuboden.

Es tagte schon als Anna aufwachte. Die Tür, in rostigen Angeln, quietschte, dann folgten Schritte auf dem Holzboden. Anna hörte Napoleon aufgeregt winseln. Die Sprossen der Leiter knarrten. Sie lag starr da. Neben ihr murmelte Hans im Schlaf. Sie schlug ihre Hände vor die weit

aufgerissenen Augen. Wieder knarrte der Boden,
dann fiel die Tür ins Schloss.

In ihrem Nachthemd stieg sie die Leiter hinunter.
Schnee klebte auf den Sprossen.

Napoleon war verschwunden. Anna wusste, dass
der Hund nur mit Peter gehen würde.

Peter! Peter! Sie würgte, wollte den geliebten
Namen schreien, aber er steckte wie ein Kloss in
ihrem Hals.

Sie sank auf die Knie und raufte sich die Haare. Sie
strich mit der Hand über die Schneespuren auf dem
Bretterboden. Gefoltert von Gewissensbissen blieb
sie wie eine Büsserin knien.

Mühsam zog sie sich an der Wand empor, schleppte
sich auf zitternden Beinen zur Tür und rannte
barfuss durch den Schnee den Fusspuren und
Pfotenabdrücken folgend. Weit oben beim Pass sah
sie zwei Umrisse, ein Mann und ein Hund. Sie

kämpften sich durch den tiefen Schnee, immer
weiter weg von ihr.

Als sie zur Hütte zurück kam war Hans
verschwunden.

Sie legte das letzte Holzscheit aufs Feuer, kniete
sich nieder und heulte wie ein verwundetes Tier.

Später nahm sie die beiden Geissen und ihren
Tragkorb und stieg ins Tal hinunter.

## Grossvaters Geistergeschichte

„Niklaus, wach auf, Du musst mit Kaplan Stockman hinauf nach Obsee um Imholz Sepp die letzte Oelung zu bringen."

Niklaus schoss auf und starrte ins Gesicht seiner Mutter. Er kreuzte seine Arme und rieb sie heftig. Dann stieg er in die Holzschuhe und zog seinen Schaffellmantel an. Mutter hielt ihm seine Mütze und Handschuhe hin. „Wenn Ihr Euch beeilt seid ihr zur Mitternachtsmesse zurück. Die Waldarbeiter haben mit den Rossen Holz vom Wald geholt, der Weg ist geräumt." Sie nahm Weihwasser aus einem Keramikgefäss, das neben der Stubentür hing, und zeichnete ein Kreuz auf Niklaus Stirn.

Niklaus wusste, dass das eine wichtige Mission war. Er war stolz, dass er als Ministrant mit dem Kaplan bis hinauf nach Obsee gehen durfte um einem

Sterbenden die letzte Oelung zu bringen, denn ohne sie konnte man nicht ins Himmelreich eingehen.

Imholz Sepp lebte das ganze Jahr auf Obsee, obwohl man eigentlich nur im Sommer auf einer Alp wohnte. Das Heimetli war im Niemandsland, es befand sich weder in Untersee noch in der Nachbarsgemeinde Melchtal.

Kaplan Stockman war jung, frisch vom Seminar, und noch nicht lange in ihrem Dorf. Er wartete auf der Kirchentreppe. Über seine Soutane hatte er einen schwarzen Umhang geworfen und er trug die Kommunion in einer kleinen Montranz. „Wir müssen uns beeilen. Vor gut einer halben Stunde war der Nachbar von Sepp hier und teilte mir mit, dass der Kranke am Sterben liege."

Niklaus schüttelte den Kopf, aber sagte nichts. Sepp hatte gar keine Nachbarn.

Ein eisiger Wind blies in sein Gesicht. Das Eis knisterte unter ihren Schuhen und es fing an zu schneien, grosse nasse Flocken. Sie landeten auf der

Laterne, glitzerten und schmolzen sofort. Seine
Handschue waren bald nass. Eiswasser trickelte
seinen Nacken hinunter und die Füsse in den
schweren Nagelschuhen waren eiskalt.

In der Schlucht fühlte es sich wärmer an, die Felsen
die sich auf beiden Seiten türmten gaben ihnen
Schutz. Sie kamen gut voran. Die Nacht war voller
Geräusche: der Melchibach, tief unten gurgelte
durch das Bachbett, Kaplan Stockman murmelte
den Rosenkranz und Tiere raschelten durch den
Schnee um sich ein Nachtlager zu suchen. Niklaus
erinnerte sich an Grossmutters Geschichte; dass an
Weihnachten die Toten zurückkommen dürfen um
ihre Versäumnisse nachzuholen und um ihre
Vergehen zu tilgen. Es war Niklaus als ob die Luft
um ihn voller Seelen war die ziellos
herumschwirrten. Es schauderte ihn vor Kälte und
Angst.

Nach der Schlucht ging es steil bergan. Der Kaplan
war sich nicht gewöhnt in den Bergen

herumzukraxeln. „Bitte, nicht so schnell, Niklaus",
keuchte er.

Niklaus verlangsamte seine Schritte und drehte sich
um. Kaplan Stockman raffte seine Soutane mit
einer Hand zusammen, in der andern balancierte er
die Monstranz. Hie und da lugte ein Halbmond
zwischen den dichten Wolken hervor. Es schneite
nicht mehr, aber von den Tannenzweigen über
ihnen regnete es Eissplitter.

Niklaus sah die Hütte von weitem. Sie stand dunkel
in der Schneelandschaft. Kein Rauch kam vom
Kamin. Die Tannen im Hintergrund schauten aus
wie Finger die gegen den Himmel zeigten. Der
kleine See war gefroren und sie wussten nicht ob sie
immer noch auf dem Pfad oder auf Eis gingen.

Beim Brunnen stellte Niklaus die Laterne ab und
zog seine Handschuhe aus. Seine Finger waren
gefroren und die Zehen schmerzten. Seine Lungen
verplatzten fast vom schnellen Gehen in der kalten
Luft.

Der Kaplan stiess die Tür auf. Die rostigen Angeln knarrten. Niklaus hob die Laterne und sah auf einem Balken eingeritzte Zahlen.

Wie von Geisterhand ging die Tür, im hinteren Teil der Hütte, auf. Die Bodenbretter knirschten als sie ins Stübli traten. Kaplan Stockman fing an zu beten: „Gott segne dieses Haus und alle die da leben." Er machte ein Kreuzzeichen. Niklaus blieb am Fussende des Bettes stehen. Ein Windstoss schlug die Türe zu. Die Kerze in der Laterne flackerte und ging aus. Sie waren im Dunkeln. Niklaus Magen machte einen Purzelbaum und seine Haut kribbelte als ob mit tausend kleiner Spinnen. Durch das schmutzige Fenster sah er wie eine Wolke den Mond freigab. Ein Lichtstrahl kroch übers Bett und beleuchtete das weisse Gesicht des Sterbenden. Schwarze Augensockel starrten gegen die Decke und dünne Finger krallten sich an das Leintuch. Imholz Sepp war seit langem krank gewesen und hatte sich von einem runden, rotbackigen Mann in ein Skelett verwandelt.

Kaplan Stockman sagte mehr Gebete, salbte den Kranken mit Oel und legte die Kommunion in den zahnlosen Mund. Er hielt die Hand des Sterbenden und mahnte Niklaus dasselbe zu tun. Er legte seine Hand auf die Finger aber zog sie schnell zurück. Sie waren so kalt.

Die Beiden konnten nicht verweilen, sie mussten schnell zurück, denn der Kaplan hatte die Mitternachtsmesse zu zelebrieren.

Zehn Minuten vor Mitternacht schlüpften die beiden durch die Sakristeitüre. Die Orgel spielte ‚Oh kommt, oh ihr Gläubigen' und Niklaus schaute in den Chor und sah dass die Kirche voll war. Er zog den roten Ministrantenrock, den ihm der Sigrist bereithielt, über.

Die Messe endete mit ‚Stille Nacht' und dann stand Kaplan Stockman beim Kirchenportal und schüttelte allen die Hand. Niklaus gesellte sich zu seinen Eltern um ihm eine ‚Frohe Weihnachten' zu wünschen. Vor ihnen stand Tante Emma, die

Klatschtante des Dorfes. Sie wusste alles: wer auf
die Welt gekommen, wer gestorben war, wer
Unartiges getrieben hatte und wer brav gewesen
war. Tante Emma schüttelte die Hand des Kaplans
eifrig. Ihr Kopftuch rutschte ihr von den schütteren
grauen Haaren, und sie sagte laut und schrill: „Man
hat mir gesagt, dass Imholz Sepp gestorben ist. Am
letzten Montag war seine Beerdigung im Melchtal.
So tragisch, dass er unterlassen hat einen Priester
zu rufen um die letzte Ölung zu bekommen." Sie
rieb eine Träne von ihrem Pergamentgesicht und
ein entsetztes Murmeln ging durch die versammelte
Gemeinde.

Der Kaplan wurde kreideweiss. Niklaus klammerte
sich an seine Mutter. Er hatte doch Sepp mit
eigenen Augen gesehen und sogar seine Hand
berührt. Wie kam es, dass sie ihn vor einigen Tagen
im Melchtal begraben hatten. Dann erinnerte sich
Niklaus  an Grossmutter. Natürlich war es Sepp
gewesen den er im Bett gesehen hatte,  sein Geist

der die Gnade erhalten hatte zurückzukommen um seine Unterlassung gut zu machen.

Niklaus schielte auf den Kaplan. Wie würde er diese Situation meistern? Der streckte seinen Arm aus und donnerte über die Menge hinweg: „Macht Euch keine Sorgen, Sepp hat die letzte Oelung erhalten, ist das nicht so Niklaus, wir gingen genau darum hinauf nach Obsee."

Niklaus nickte und stammelte, „mo mol, genau darum." Auch er sagte weder Zeit noch Tag.

Und plötzlich, inmitten der Leute, entdeckte er ein abgemagertes Gesicht und einen Mund der sich zu einem Lächeln verzog.

## Die Wallfahrt

Die Bergstrasse, die sich am Rand einer Schlucht entlang zog, war in schlechtem Zustand, ausgewaschen von zu viel Regen und Schnee. Gestein rollte den Abhang hinunter in den Melchibach, der sich schäumend durch Felsen und Baumstämme stürzte. In einer besonders steilen Kurve sackten die hinteren Räder des Postautos ab. Staub wirbelte auf und Schotter prasselte am Chassis hoch. Paul zuckte zusammen.

Es war gut fünfzig Jahre her, seit er in seinen Sonntagschuhen auf dieser Strasse mehr geschlittert als gerannt war, um im Tal unten die Bahnverbindung nach Luzern, Basel und weiter nach Rotterdam nicht zu verpassen. Im Hafen hatte er sich ein Schiffsbillet der dritten Klasse über den Atlantik gekauft. Die Reise führte ihn nach Kanada, in die weiten Ebenen von Manitoba, dem versprochenen Land.

Paul und eine Bäuerin, in einem geblümtem Sommerkleid, waren die einzigen Fahrgäste im Postauto. Sie starrte ihn an als ob sie ihn kennen müsste, zuckte dann aber die Schultern und wandte ihren Blick ab. Für sie war er ein Fremder, ein Tourist im fortgeschrittenen Alter, in Manchesterhosen und kariertem Hemd.

Er wischte die verstaubte Scheibe mit seinem Hemdärmel sauber. Bauernhöfe klebten an den Abhängen. Nadelholzwälder führten hinauf zu den zerklüfteten Felsen und den Geröllhalden, hinauf zu den Granitgipfeln, die in den tiefblauen Himmel ragten.

Die vielen Kehrtwendungen liessen Paul schwindlig werden. Erleichtert atmete er auf, als sie endlich auf dem Postplatz von Untersee Halt machten. Er nahm seinen Rucksack und den Wanderstock und stieg aus. Ein schläfriger Hund hob den Kopf und spitzte die Ohren. Ein paar Hühner scharrten im Kies und eine alte Frau, ein Tuch um den Kopf gebunden, hinkte der Kirche zu.

Paul breitete seine Arme aus und atmete die klare
Luft tief in seine Lungen. Am liebsten wäre er auf
die Erde gekniet um sie zu küssen. Sein Blick
schweifte hinauf über Matten und zerfurchte
Felsen, hinauf zu seinen Bergen.

In Kanada war der Horizont grenzenlos. Himmel
nichts als Himmel. Hier, in seiner Heimat,
herrschten die Berge, man musste sie erklimmen
um mehr vom Firmament zu sehen. Sein Hals
verengte sich; seine Augen schmerzten. All das
hatte er vermisst. Je älter er wurde umso mehr
waren die Erinnerungen an seine Kindheit und
Jugendzeit zu einem Schmerz tief in seinem
Inneren geworden.

„Ich alter Trottel!" Er schüttelte sich.

Eine mit Kopfstein gepflasterte Gasse führte
zwischen verwitterten Häusern zur Kirche hinauf.
Vom Schulhaus kam der monotone Gesang der
Schüler, die das Einmaleins aufsagten.
Generationen von Kinder waren hier, mehr oder

weniger freiwillig, zur Schule gegangen. Er hatte zu den Letzteren gehört.

Hinter der Kirche stand sein ehemaliges Elternhaus. Ein kleines Haus, überschattet von mächtigen Fichten. Paul wischte sich mit dem Handrücken die Stirn ab.

Gottlob, das Haus war nicht modernisiert worden. Die kleinen Butzenscheiben glänzten in der Morgensonne. Die Spalten in den Holzbalken waren tiefer und das Dach hatte einige Schindel verloren, aber sonst war alles beim alten. Wer war wohl jetzt der Eigentümer? Seine Familie lebte schon seit langem nicht mehr hier. Die Eltern waren schon lange tot und sein Bruder wohnte in Zürich.

Paul schaute auf die Kirchenuhr. Es war noch früh. Er hatte es nicht mehr ausgehalten im Hotel in Luzern und hatte den Frühzug genommen.

Er schaute den Abhang hinauf. Weiter oben sah er den steinigen Pfad, wie er in der Schlucht verschwand um sich später zwischen Felsblöcken hinauf zur Geröllhalde zu schlängeln. Eine Kraft zog ihn. Er musste gehen. Die Alp war seine Verantwortung, sein Erbteil, aber er hatte sich nie darum gekümmert, konnte sich nicht mal an den Namen seines Pächters erinnern. Sein Bruder hatte nach dem Rechten gesehen und ihm den Zins pünktlich auf sein Bankkonto überwiesen.

Ein scharfer Wind fuhr ihm durch die schütteren Haare. Wolken türmten sich um das Gebirge. Hier, in dieser Gegend, kamen die Gewitter vom Westen. Nebelfetzen krochen vom Tal hinauf den Hängen entlang.

Paul zögerte. Vielleicht sollte er sich nicht so weit hinaufwagen. Vielleicht sollte er im Gasthaus einen Kaffee trinken und dann wieder zurück nach Luzern fahren. Er hatte seine Pflicht getan. Zuerst hatte er im Tal unten das Grab seiner Eltern besucht und da für eine Weile gebetet. Jetzt stand er vor dem Haus in dem er aufgewachsen war. Was wollte er mehr? Aber nein, es liess ihm keine Ruhe, er musste diesen Gang wagen.

Die Wolken hatten sich noch mehr verdichtet. Hoffentlich liess der Regen noch auf sich warten. Der Pfad über die Geröllhalde könnte gefährlich werden, rutschig oder sogar unmöglich zu begehen. Paul zog seine Windjacke aus dem Rucksack und ein braunes Kuvert flatterte auf den Boden. ‚Nur für den Adressat‘, stand klar und deutlich darauf. Er verzog sein Gesicht und stopfte den Umschlag mit zitternden Händen in den Rucksack zurück, hob seinen Stock auf und nahm den Weg unter die Füsse. Eine Stunde hinauf, eine halbe Stunde hinunter, das hat er als Bub geleistet, heute würde er länger brauchen.

Paul machte gute Fortschritte. „Ha, dieser alte Hund ist noch lange nicht tot", rief er und ballte die Faust. „He, Sensemann, du kannst mich noch nicht haben."

Der Pfad bog leicht ab und führte um einen riesigen Felsblock in die Schlucht. Es roch nach Moos und vermoderten Bäumen. Tief unten schäumte der Bach durch Steinbrocken und entwurzelte Bäume. Sie sahen aus wie Skelette prähistorischer Tiere.

In der Entfernung rollte der erste Donner und vom Dorf hörte Paul die Angelus- Glocke. Er bekreuzigte sich.

In Kanada hatte die Arbeit den Vorrang gehabt, das Gebet kam zuletzt. Zuerst hatte er als Knecht auf einem Hof geschuftet, dann hatte er eine Farm gekauft, baute Getreide an und verdiente viel Geld. Nun hatten seine Söhne das Geschäft übernommen, seine Frau war tot, und er fühlte sich auf dem Abstellgeleise.

Paul setzte die Füsse vorsichtig auf. Er brauchte die Steine als Treppe. Gelegentlich hielt er an und schnaufte schwer, sein Hals eng, sein Herz wild schlagend. Vorgebeugt, mit den Händen auf die Knie gestützt, schnappte er nach Luft.

Kaum war er aus der Schlucht, begann die Ueberquerung des Geröllfeldes. Rinnsale sprangen aus Ritzen zwischen dem Schiefer und machten die Platten glitschig. Weit oben pfiffen die Murmeltiere ihre Warnung und Adler kreisten über den schroffen Felsen.

Paul setzte sich hinter einen windgeschützten Stein. Sonnenstrahlen drangen durch die Wolken und beleuchteten weit unten im Tal die Dächer des Dorfes und den Kupferturm der Kirche. Blitze durchzuckten den Himmel. Dunkle Schatten glitten über die Abhänge.

Seine Augenlider flackerten und der Kopf fiel ihm auf die Brust. Als er wieder erwachte war es fast dunkel. Es blitzte und der Donner liess nicht lang auf sich warten; das Gewitter würde bald über ihm sein. Er musste sich schnellstens auf den Weg machen. Im Notfall konnte er auf der Alp übernachten. Die Nieuw Amsterdam verliess Rotterdam erst in einer Woche und er hatte dem Fräulein am Hotelempfang in Luzern gesagt, dass er eventuell ein oder zwei Nächte wegbleiben würde.

Als Paul das Plateau erreichte, platzten die ersten
Regentropfen auf den staubigen Pfad. Er sah die
Alphütte am anderen Ende des kleinen Sees. Sie
kauerte wie ein altes Riesentier am Abhang. Rauch
schlängelte aus dem Kamin. Er wanderte dem See
entlang. Gewitterwolken spiegelten sich im Wasser
und Wellen schlugen ans Ufer.

Er schluckte trocken und strich sich mit der Hand
über seine feuchten Augen. Seine Familie hatte den
ganzen Sommer hier oben gewohnt. Es war ein
hartes Leben gewesen, aber auch ein schönes. Als er
älter wurde, hatte er Pläne gemacht, die Alphütte,
sein Erbgut, in einen Bauernhof umzubauen und
endlich das Land richtig zu bewirtschaften aber sein
Vater wollte nichts davon wissen, hatte nur gelacht
und mit dem Finger an die Stirn getippt. Sie hatten
einen schlimmen Streit und Paul wurde  bewusst,
dass hier nicht Platz für sie beide war. Darum war
er nach Kanada ausgewandert. In den weiten

Ebenen würde das Bauern viel leichter sein, so hatte er gedacht. Ja, das war es sicher, aber wie hatte er all das hier vermisst.

Das näherkommende Gebimmel von Kuhglocken weckte ihn aus seinen Gedanken. Mit dem Stolz eines Bauern schaute er auf die grosse Herde, die sich an ihm vorbeidrängte. Trotz des strömenden Regens erkannte er den  Schmuggelpfad der sich zum Pass hinaufwand.

Im Schutz des überhängenden Hüttendaches erhob sich ein Berner Sennenhund und bellte.

„Ruhig Barry", rief eine Stimme und ein Mann trat über die Türschwelle. „Grüezi."

„Grüezi", anwortete Paul und fügte bei, „kann ich im Heu übernachten?"

Der Aelpler strich sich durch die Mähne seines weissen Haares und verzog den Mund zu einem Schmunzeln. „Sicher, kommt rein. Hier in den

Bergen dauern die Unwetter. Heute wird es klöpfen."

Wie zur Bestätigung riss ein Blitz den Himmel entzwei, gefolgt von ohrenbetäubendem Donner.

„Dort, geht mal an die Wärme, ihr seid ja ganz nass." Er zeigte mit seiner Pfeife auf das prasselnde Feuer im Kamin.

Die beiden Männer sassen auf wackligen Stabellen. Der Hund lag ausgestreckt auf Pauls Füssen. Er streichelte sein zottiges Fell. Sie redeten kaum. Sein ganzes Leben hatte er schwer daran getan Floskeln von sich zu geben und war froh über die Stille. Sie hörten dem Donner zu der die Hütte bis aufs Fundament rüttelte. Das Licht des Feuers erhellte den grossen Raum mit einer Eckbank und einem Tisch am anderen Ende. Die Tür zum Stübli stand offen und er sah das Bett mit der rot-weiss karierten Decke. Eine Leiter führte auf den Heuboden, der die ganze Länge der Hütte und des angebauten Stalles einnahm.

Regenschübe prasselten an die Fenster und aufs Schieferdach. Fensterläden trommelten an die Holzbalken.

Sie setzten sich an den Tisch und assen eine einfache Mahlzeit: selbstgemachten Käse und Brot, getrocknetes Fleisch und eine grosse Henkeltasse Milchkaffee.

„He du, du bisch doch der Imholz Päuli?" Der Senn zeigte mit seiner schwieligen Hand auf Paul.

„Ja, öppa scho, und du bisch de Rohrer Uli? Wir sind doch Jahrgänger, oder?"

Uli verzog sein gefurchtes Gesicht. „He, jo, und wir machten die Gegend unsicher mit unseren Schelmenstücken."

Paul war immer gut ausgekommen mit Uli.  Sie hatten ein paar Balgereien und waren hie und da mit knapper Not dem Zorn von Vater oder dem Lineal von Schwester Dolores, ihrer Lehrerin,

entkommen. Wie  hatten sie sich dann ins
Fäustchen gelacht.

„Dir gehört die Alp", sagte Uli. „Ich hab meinen
Zins immer pünktlich bezahlt, jeden Martini bin ich
extra nach Zürich gefahren, um deinem Bruder
höchstpersönlich..."

Paul unterbrach ihn. „Mo mol, du bist ein guter
Pächter, ich kann mich nicht beklagen."

Uli fing an zu husten, ein tiefsitzender,
brustzerreissender Husten, und fuhr sich mit dem
Hemdärmel über den Mund. „Das ist mein letzter
Sommer hier oben. Wills Gott kann ich noch bis
Ende September durchhalten." Er zeigte auf die
geschnitzten Zahlen im Balken. „Meine Tage sind
gezählt."

Paul nickte. Er wusste wie es Uli zumute war. Bei
ihm war es zuerst das Rheuma das sich bemerkbar
gemacht hatte und dann dieser andere Schmerz der
an ihm nagte. Heute Abend würde er den Brief
öffnen. Er war sonst kein Feigling, aber das hatte er

für zu lange aufgeschoben. Wer wollte schon sein Todesurteil schwarz auf weiss lesen?

Später sass er oben auf dem Heuboden und riss schweren Herzens den Umschlag auf. Beim Licht einer Taschenlampe las er, was endlich gelesen werden musste.

Er schnaufte laut auf, hob seinen Kopf und starrte auf die Dachbalken. „Dank dir, lieber Gott", sagte er laut und bekreuzte sich. Der Befund war nicht eindeutig. Er konnte damit leben, musste es nicht unbedingt wissen.

In der Nacht hörte Paul dem Regen zu. Um ihn seufzten die Balken und das Heu wisperte. Fünfzig Jahre waren vergangen, aber er sah alles deutlich vor sich.

Der Vater arbeitete den ganzen Tag: Er mähte Grass, flickte Zäune und Steinmauern oder besserte die Hütte aus.

Jeden Abend rief er den Betruf durch den
Holztrichter, und der Ruf hallte von den anderen
Alpen wider. Die Klänge eines Alphorns stimmten
in das gesungene Gebet ein. Der Abendwind strich
durch die Tannen und die Berge färbten sich rot.

Paul und sein Bruder jodelten, während sie die
Kühe molken und wetteiferten, wer Mutter mehr
Milch in die Hütte bringen konnte. Diese hatte
ihren Rock geschürzt, die Aermel aufgerollt, und
die kastanienfarbenen Haare mit einem Kopftuch
zurückgebunden. Mit einem Handgriff schwang sie
das Kessi über die Glut, um die Milch zu Käse zu
verarbeiten.

Am Abend sassen sie auf der Bank unter dem
überhängenden Dach und gingen durch das
Alphabet. Mutter hielt grosse Stücke auf eine gute
Bildung.

Wenn es regnete und das Melken getan war,
schnitzten die beiden Buben an irgendeinem
Holzstück oder schrieben Rechnungen oder

Aufsätze in ihre Hefte, während Mutter Socken und Pullover flickte. Bei gutem Wetter kletterten sie die Felswände hinauf oder schwammen über den Gletschersee, um einander zu beweisen wie tapfer sie waren.

Seufzend hob Paul seinen Kopf und zog die Wolldecke höher.

Sein Herz schmerzte, als er an seine kleine Schwester dachte. Sie war nicht einmal ein Jahr alt gewesen als sie an den Masern starb. Vater hatte den kleinen Sarg aus roh gezimmerten Brettern zusammengenagelt. Drei Tage war ihr wächserner Körper in der Hütte aufgebahrt.

„Gott gibt und Gott nimmt." Die Stimme seiner Mutter hatte tapfer aber so unendlich traurig geklungen.

Sonnenstrahlen fielen durch die Dachluke und weckten Paul. Er stiess sie auf und schaute hinaus. Vor ihm lagen die Alpenwiesen. Dies war sein Reich, das er einfach so weggeworfen und vernachlässigt hatte. Die Berge strahlten und spiegelten sich im Bergsee. Die Kühe grasten auf den alten festgestampften Pfaden bis hinauf zum Pass. Nach dem Regen der letzten Nacht sah alles wie frisch gewaschen aus.

Paul reckte sich. Diese ganze Geschichte mit seiner Gesundheit hatte ihn aufhorchen lassen. Er würde nicht ewig leben, er wusste nicht, was um die Ecke auf ihn wartete.

„Nur das Jetzt zählt, reg dich, es geht an die Arbeit.“ Paul lachte vor sich hin und kletterte die Leiter runter.

Er hatte Uli schon früh rumoren gehört. Die Kühe waren gemolken, das Holz gespalten und die Milch kochte im Kessi über dem Feuer. Frisch aufgebrühter Kaffee und ein grosser Laib Brot standen auf dem Tisch.

Paul gesellte sich zu Uli, der neben dem Feuer sass und seine Pfeife stopfte. Er räusperte sich und kam schnurstracks zur Sache. „Willst, dass ich bleibe?

Ich kann dir helfen. Zusammen schaffen wir es." Er zerriss den Brief und warf ihn in die Glut.

Als ob er eine Kuh kaufen würde, schaute ihn Uli von oben bis unten an, klemmte sich die Pfeife zwischen die Zähne, grinste schräg, und nickte.

## Der Besuch

Sammy boxte die Luft. „Dort ist es, ha!" Er zeigte
auf das Bauernhaus auf der andern Seite des Sees.
Rauch wirbelte aus dem Kamin.

Hinter dem Haus führten Wiesen hinauf zu den
Felsen und Bergen die mit dem ersten Schnee
bedeckt waren. Ein enger Pfad wand sich dem Pass
zu.

Lisa runzelte die Stirn. „Besten Dank, dass du uns
hier hinauf geschleppt hast und dazu noch auf
diesem, was, ha, ha, Wanderweg. Warum nicht die
Strasse? Du hast uns fast in den Tod gestürzt auf
diesem Geissenpfad und jetzt verschanzt du uns
hier oben." Sie stiess Sammy in den Rücken. „Dein
Plan ist total verrückt. Was wenn er dich kennt?"

Ziva stützte die Hände auf ihre Knie und keuchte:
„Genau, Lisa hat recht. Du bist verdammt
unvorsichtig, einfach..."

„Keine Sorge." Sammy unterbrach Ziva und drehte sich um. Lisa schaute ihn erschrocken an. Er war weiss wie der Tod. Sah aus wie ein Vampier, aber ohne die langen Zähne. Lisa machte sich Sorgen um seine Gesundheit, den Husten der ihn in der Nacht plagte.

Sammy schwang seine Arme. „Der kennt mich nicht, hat mich nie mehr gesehen seit ich ein Kid war. Wir haben keine Wahl, wir müssen irgendwo untertauchen, wenn auch nur für einige Tage."

Lisa legte die flache Hand unter ihre Nase. „Wisst ihr was? Ich habe es bis oben hin mit all diesem Shit." Der kalte Wind liess sie erschauern.

Sie liefen dem See entlang und Sammy kickte Steine ins Wasser. Wellen rieselten über das kiesige Ufer. Sammys Haare hingen in Strähnen über den Kragen des langen schwarzen Mantels der wie die Flügel eines mystischen Vogels um seine Beine schlug.

Lisa und Ziva versuchten ihn einzuholen. „Hey big guy", rief Lisa. "Es machte uns wirklich Spass das Auto zu stehlen und du warst gut! Wie ein Profi bist du durch all den Verkehr gefahren." Ziva flatterte ihre Hände in Samuels Gesicht . „Oh ja, und  als wir den Mercedes über den Felsen in die Schlucht hinunter stiessen, das war der Hammer. All das Metal auf einem Haufen."

Lisa schaute Ziva an. Sie war eine gute Freundin, alles wollte sie immer recht machen. Sie schaute ihr zu wie sie, schwach mit Magersucht, torkelte als ob sie betrunken wäre, sich aber jedesmal wieder aufraffte.

Sie ähnelten sich wie Zwillinge. Beide trugen Schottenminis,  Lederjacken und Doc Martins. Ihre pechschwarzen Haare waren geflochten.

Imholz Leo stand unter der Haustür und schützte seine tränenden Augen vor dem grellen Licht. Er hatte die drei Wanderer, die dem See entlang kamen, schon seit einiger Zeit beobachtet.

Er nahm seinen Stock und hinkte in den Hof hinaus. Hie und da war es gut mit jemand zu plaudern.

Leo schaute an seinem Bauernhof hoch. Sein Vetter, Paul Imholz , war als reicher Mann aus Kanada zurückgekommen und hatte die einfache Alphütte in dieses stolze Haus umgebaut. Für einige Jahre hatte Päuli hier oben glücklich und zufrieden gewohnt. Er hatte sogar Weizen angepflanzt. Alle Leute waren erstaunt als er starb. Das Haus wurde verpachtet und als Gasthof geführt und einige Jahre später entschlossen sich seine Buben in Kanada, ihm, Leo, den Hof spotbillig anzubieten.

Leo hatte Schwein gehabt. Und dann baute die Forstkommission eine Strasse und machte es leichter hier hinauf zu kommen. Ja, er liebte sein Leben hier in den Bergen, aber manchmal hätte er schon gern Nachbarn gehabt. Seine Tochter besuchte ihn so gut wie nie, und wenn sie mal kam versuchte sie ihn zu überreden den Hof auf ihren Namen zu überschreiben. Sie war eine Gerissene, er traute ihr nicht. Er rieb sich die Nase. Nun, er würde das letzte Wort haben.

Es nachtete bald. Die Sonne war hinter den Bergen verschwunden und rote und gelbe Streifen durchkreuzten den Himmel.

Mit weit ausgestreckten Armen fingen die drei Wanderer an zu laufen.

Leo nickte. Das waren keine Wanderer, das waren Teenagers, ganz und gar nicht zum Wandern gekleidet. Er war nicht ganz weltfremd, er las die Zeitung, die ihm der Postbote einmal in der Woche brachte, gründlich durch. Das waren Punks oder so was ähnliches.

Der junge Mann war offensichtlich der Anführer. Er sprach durch zusammengepresste Zähne. „Wir bleiben für eine Weile", marschierte zur Haustüre und winkte den Mädchen ihm zu folgen.

Als Leo in die Küche kam, sassen die drei schon auf der Eckbank hinter dem Küchentisch. Dem jungen Mann ging es offensichtlich nicht gut. Er hielt den Kopf in beiden Händen, das Gesicht war das eines Kindes, mit dem Schatten eines Bartes. Irgendwie glich er jemand. Nein, er hatte diese jungen Leute noch nie gesehen. Das waren Nichtsnutze, von Luzern vermutlich. Was wollten sie? Wollten sie sich hier wohl einnisten? Aber warum? Warum bei einem alten Mann mit ein paar Kühen. Die hatten irgend was verbrochen, darum mussten sie sich verstecken. Leo beherbergte Wanderer wenn das Wetter sich verschlechterte, er würde auch mit dieser Jungmannschaft zurecht kommen.

Ein Windstoss rüttelte an den Fensterläden und blies ins Kamin. Die Glut knisterte und hisste.

Eines der Mädchen legte die Beine auf den Tisch. „Hast Du was zu trinken, ich meine nicht Tee oder Kaffee, verdammi, ich meine Schnaps.“

Leo zuckte zusammen. Diese jungen Leute waren so
frech. Aber er brauchte sich nicht zu fürchten, sie
waren nichts als Kinder. Irgendwie verstand er sie.
Die Jungen hatten es nicht leicht heutzutage, sie
kamen zu nichts. Wenigstens würde sein Grosskind,
Samuel, einmal ein Haus besitzen.

Er, Leo, hatte ein gutes Leben hinter sich. Er hatte
früh geheiratet und er und seine Mathilda, Gott hab
sie selig, waren  glücklich gewesen. Obgleich er
seinen Enkel für Jahre nicht gesehen hatte, würde
er ihm alles vermachen. Wenn er nicht hier leben
wollte konnte er ja das Bauerhaus verpachten oder
verkaufen.

„Ich heisse Leo, Imholz Leo, wie heisst ihr drei?"
Leo sass auf seinem dreibeinigen Melchstuhl und
stopfte seine Pfeife.

„Das braucht niemand zu wissen." Schüttelfrost
schien den jungen Mann zu plagen. Eines der
Mädchen streichelte seinen Arm. Leo nahm eine
Wolldecke von der Bank und legte sie ihm über die

Schultern. Der Junge schaute ihn mit grossen blauen Augen an. Augen die er kennen sollte, Augen die kindlich und verletzlich waren.

„Gibt's hier was zu essen für meine Freunde?" Das Mädchen, das aussah wie ein Skelett, rumorte im Küchenschrank. Sie nahm eine Schachtel Guetzli und ein Laib Käse vom Regal und warf die Esswaren auf den Tisch. Sie fanden den Schnaps den Leo für seine Kühe brauen durfte wenn sie kalberten. Sie reichten eine der Flaschen herum und husteten und spuckten.

„Was bedeuten die komischen Zahlen auf dem Balken im Gang, das sieht richtig gespenstisch aus." Der junge Mann versuchte sich zu unterhalten, dachte Leo, vielleicht tat es ihm leid, dass er und die Mädchen sich so unanständig aufgeführt hatten.

Leo wusste nicht was die Zahlen bedeuteten. Ja richtig, er hatte sie auch immer als unheimlich empfunden und wollte sie sogar einmal aushobeln.

Später gingen die jungen Leute hinauf in eines der
Zimmer. Leo schlief in einem alten Stuhl neben
dem Herd ein.

In der Nacht weckte ihn das laute Husten des
Buben und besorgte Stimmen. Es nahm ihn wunder
was dem Jungen fehlte, vielleicht hatten sie in
feuchten Orten übernachtet oder...?

Stimmen weckten ihn. Er hinkte zur Türe. Zwei
Bergsteiger mit schweren Rucksäcken wünschten
ihm einen guten Morgen und verschwanden gegen
den Pass. Hätte er etwas sagen sollen? Vielleicht
hätten die beiden Männer für ihn die Polizei
verständigt. Seine Besucher waren vielleicht doch
gefährlich.

Nicht daran denken. Jetzt zuerst die Kühe melken.

Auf dem Weg zurück vom Stall musste er sich gegen
den Türbalken lehnen. Sein Herz schlug wie rasend.
Ein fürchterlicher Schmerz übermannte ihn,
presste seine Brust zusammen, immer enger.
Langsam glitt er auf den Boden hinunter, sass da

und rang nach Luft. Dies passierte ihm bald jeden Tag. Er raffte sich auf und hinkte langsam hinauf zum ersten Stock. Alle drei hatten sich im grossen Bett eingenistet. Sie sahen aus wie Kinder. Eines der Mädchen saugte an ihrem Daumen, das andere drehte an einer Haarsträhne. Der Junge lag zusammengerollt wie ein Igel. Endlich schlief er.

Lisa erwachte zuerst. Der Duft von frischem Brot und Kaffee hatte sie geweckt. Sie war wieder ein Kind, daheim bei ihren Eltern, sie schmiegte sich in ihre Kuscheldecke. Sie war so müde. Sie hatte genug von diesem Leben, immer auf der Strasse und hie und da besetzten sie so ein shittiges Haus. Und nach ihrem letzten Streich würden sie sicher im Käfig landen. Die Polizei würde sie finden. Sie wollte heimgehen, sie wollte ihre Mutter sehen.

Lisa bewunderte den alten Mann, er war super cool, er hatte total keine Angst vor ihnen und behandelte sie wie normal.

Sie schlich die Stiege hinunter. Sie wollte mit Leo sprechen, bevor die andern aufwachten, sie wollte ihm sagen, dass sie ihm nichts tun würden. Ja, Sammy war viel hässig, aber es ging ihm nicht gut. Auch war er total verbittert wegen seiner Mutter die immer betrunken war und sein angeblicher Vater der nach Amerika abgedampft war. Sie wollte Leo sagen – und sie wusste das von ihrer Grossmutter wie wichtig das für die ältere Generation war – Sammy fluchte nie, er sprach immer mit einer ganz vornehmen Stimme und er war clever. Er war nicht wie sie und Ziva, bei ihnen war es immer Shit dies und Shit das.

Sie stolperte. „Verdammt noch mal, was..?" Die ersten Strahlen der Morgensonne erhellten die Küche. Der alte Mann lag auf dem Boden. Seine Augen starrten gegen die Decke. Sie fühlte seinen Puls. Imholz Leo war tot. Lisa zog sich an den Haaren und schrie. Ziva und Samuel rannten die Stiege hinunter. Sie starrten auf den Toten und auf den Tisch der für drei gedeckt war, auf das frisch gebackene Brot, die Konfi und die Kaffeekanne. Es schien als ob Leo sie zum Essen rufen wollte.

Die zwei Mädchen schluchzten und Samuel fiel auf die Knie und umarmte Leo. Er schmiegte sein Gesicht an das seines Grossvaters und schluchzte.

# Der Schneesturm

Untersee, Weihnachten 1993

Mein lieber Charles,

jetzt da ich endlich eine Entscheidung getroffen habe, greife ich zur Feder um mein langjähriges Versprechen zu erfüllen. Ich will Dir einen Einblick in das Erlebnis meiner Jugend geben, das mich so gravierend prägte.

Das Schreiben ist die einzige Gefährtin die mir geblieben ist, meine Muse. Tagaus, tagein gehe ich, in einen abgewetzten Morgenmantel gekleidet, hin und her und warte auf sie.

Als mein Verleger in England weisst Du, lieber Charles, dass ich einige Bücher geschrieben habe. Aber warum konnte ich nie zu Papier bringen was damals geschah, meine Erinnerungen, sie spielen andauernd Verstecken, ich konnte sie nie in Worte fassen.

Warum? Aus meiner Mutters Grab vernehme ich immer noch ihre Stimme: „Sohn, gib acht was du schreibst."

Und nun lade ich Dich ein, lieber Charles, mich nach Obsee in die Schweizer Berge zu begleiten.

1959, als ich 12 Jahre alt war, entschloss sich Vater, dass wir Weihnachten in Obsee verbringen würden. Ich legte den Kopf auf meine verschränkten Arme und seufzte. Es war ein Ort, wo Hasen und Füchse sich Gute Nacht sagen. Das einzige was ich daran mochte, war die Bahnfahrt von Zürich mit der SBB. Mutter sprach Worte des Trostes und mein Vater sah über seine Brillenränder hinweg und befahl ihr ruhig zu sein.

Ich kannte Obsee nur zu gut von unseren Ferien im vergangenen Sommer. Die Berge glichen den verfaulten Zähnen prähistorischer Monster. Der See war zu kalt zum Schwimmen und die Felsen zu schlüpfrig zum Klettern. Kühe, mit grossen Schellen, grassten ziellos an den Abhängen. Alphütten duckten sich im kurzen Stoppelgrass, und das einzige Haus war der Gasthof Obsee wo wir von Herrn und Frau Trun beherbergt wurden.

Noch heute überkommt es mich kalt wenn ich an unsere Ankuft im letzten Postauto, bei dickem Eisnebel, zurückdenke.

Herr Trun tauchte aus dem Schatten auf. Sein Buckel war unter einer Wolldecke versteckt. Er lud unsere Koffer auf den Motorschlitten und meine Eltern setzten sich neben ihn. Ich kauerte mit dem Gepäck auf dem Notsitz. Unser Fahrer handhabte das Steuerrad so als ob er mit dem Geweih eines aufsässigen wilden Rehes zu  kämpfen hätte, und wir stoben in einer Wolke von Schnee davon.

Meine Mutter klammerte sich an Vater aber der schob sie weg.

Als wir aus der Nebelgrenze kamen, schimmerten die Berge in der Abendsonne. Weisse Schneefelder führten hinunter zum gefrorenen See.

Das traditionelle Schweizerhaus mit überhängendem Dach und grünen Fensterläden stand wie ein schwarzer Scherenschnitt am weissen Abhang. Graue Wolken mit gelben Rändern begannen sich aufzutürmen und verkündeten noch mehr Schnee. Vielleicht würden wir für Wochen eingeschneit sein.

Die Wände und Decken des Hauses waren holzverkleidet. Rot-weiss karierte Vorhänge verzierten die Fenster und im Kamin loderte ein Feuer das tanzende Schatten an die Wände warf.

„Das Nachtessen ist punkt sechs", sagte Frau Trun. Unsere Gastgeber waren eindrucksvoll. Sie war dick wie ein Fass und er war dünn wie eine Gerte. Sie war langsam und bedächtig. Er war flink zu Fuss und im Aufbrausen. Einmal hatte ich beobachtet wie ein Küchenmesser im Türrahmen landete.

Ich bekam immer den gleichen Verschlag unter dem Dach, während meine Eltern ein grosses Zimmer, mit Kachelofen, im ersten Stock hatten.

Der einzige andere Gast im Speisezimmer war eine Frau mit prächtigen roten Haaren. Ihre Haut war weiss wie Schnee, und sie schaute mich mit dunkeln Augen an, oder war es Vater, den sie anstarrte. Es gab Fisch und Bratkartoffeln die uns Herr Trun, seine Wolldecke durch eine weisse Kellnerjacke ersetzt, servierte. Ich versteckte mich hinter meiner Serviette und tupfte meinen Mund nach jedem Bissen ab. Als ich mein Lieblingsdessert ass – Schokoladen Schaum – konnte ich endlich den Blick der Dame vergessen.

Vater stellte uns vor: „Herr und Frau Baumann und Herbert, unser Sohn. Wir kommen aus Zürich."

In der Schweiz tat man sich dazumal schwer mit Vornamen ausser man war ein Kind. So war ich Herbert, ein mir verhasster Name. Ich stellte mich manchmal als Clark Gable vor, das war soviel besser.

Sie hiess Frau Krähenfuss und war am Nachmittag von Frankfurt angereist.

Krähenfuss! Ich verdeckte mein Gesicht mit der Hand und kicherte.

Vater stiess mich in die Seite, aber wandte seinen Blick nicht von ihr. Er fragte: „Sind sie allein?"

Sie nickte. „Ja, heute Nacht." Sie betonte heute Nacht. „Mein Mann kommt morgen in Begleitung von zwei Bekannten." Sie lächelte. „Und einem kleinen Freund für dich, Herbert."

„Was?" Ich schluckte trocken. Das war das Letzte was ich brauchte, einen Fratz zu dem ich schauen musste.

„Freut dich das nicht?" Ihr Gesicht kam so nahe, dass ich ihre langen Spinnenwimpern und Krähenfüsse sah.

Sie kicherte wie ein Hexe. „Oh Mann! Ich wusste nicht, dass heute ein Pferderennen stattfindet."

Ich wusste sofort, dass sie meine vorstehenden Zähne meinte, warf meine Serviette auf den Tisch und ballte meine Faust.

Vater lachte laut und Mutter legte ihren Arm um mich. Ich presste mein Gesicht an ihre Brust und fühlte ihr Herz wild schlagen. Ich befreite mich und rannte hinauf in mein Zimmer.

Ich konnte nicht schlafen. Um Mitternacht erhob ich mich und schlich auf Zehenspitzen ans Dachfenster. Ein unheimlicher Nebel voll wild tanzender Sterne hatte uns eingehüllt. Es schneite.

Obwohl ich ein ängstlicher Bub war, nahm ich meine Taschenlampe, stieg die wacklige Stiege hinunter und klopfte ans Zimmer meiner Eltern. Niemand antwortete. Es war verschlossen. Unter der gegenüberliegenden Tür sah ich einen Lichtstreifen. Das Zimmer von Frau Krähenfuss. Ich drehte den Knauf und die Tür bewegte sich.

Mein Vater war alles andere als langsam, sei es bei unseren ständig wechselnden Dienstmädchen oder weiblichen Bekannten. Und zu allem hatte er meine Mutter in ihr Zimmer eingeschlossen. Wie konnte er nur? Im Rhythmus des quietschenden Bettes schlug ich meinen Kopf an den Türrahmen.

Am Morgen hatte sich der Schneesturm gelegt. Ich stieg von meinem Zimmer herunter und gesellte mich zu meinen Eltern die bereits frühstückten. Vater goss den Kaffee ein und Mutter strich die Brote mit Butter und Konfitüre. „Einen frohen Heiligabend." Sie tätschelte meinen Arm. Ich lehnte mich an sie.

„Hast du gut geschlafen, Kind", fragte Vater. Ich hasste es wenn er mich Kind nannte.

Im Vergleich zu gestern Abend wirkte das Gesicht von Frau Krähenfuss nackt. Sie war ausser sich. „Frau Trun hat mich soeben davon unterrichtet, dass die Strasse hinunter ins Dorf mit Schnee blockiert ist." Sie rieb sich die Augen. „Wir sind abgeschnitten. Mein Mann und unsere Freunde werden die Festtage in Untersee verbringen müssen."

Ich atmete auf. Kein Zaupf, der mir Weihnachten verdarb.

Als ich Vater von der Seite ansah, bemerkte ich einen Schimmer in seinen Augen. Nicht sein anzüglicher Blick, eher ein ritterlicher und fester. „Kein Problem, das bisschen Schnee soll uns nicht aufhalten. Herr Trun wird mir seinen Schlitten leihen und wir holen sie vom Postauto ab." Es fehlte nicht viel und Vater hätte wie ein Pfadfinder salutiert.

Krähenfuss legte eine manikürierte Hand auf Vaters Arm. „Wunderbar, sie kommen am Nachmittag in Untersee an."

Nach dem Frühstück entfloh ich hinaus in den Schnee. Dicke Wolken verdeckten die Berge. Herr Trun winkte mich mit seinen krallenartigen Fingern zu sich. „Komm, hilf mir mit dem Weihnachtsbaum."

Er schob den Motorschlitten aus dem Schober. Der Schneepflug pflügte den Schnee beidseitig zu hohen Wächten. Beim Tannenwäldchen hielten wir an, und unser Wirt hinkte zu einer der Tannen und fällte sie mit einem Beil.

Damals war ich an allem Mechanischen interessiert. Der Schlitten bestand aus einem alten Kabriolet, die vorderen Räder auf Kufen montiert. Ich strich meine Hand über das komische Gefährt. Ich kniete nieder, schaute drunter und nickte.

Während des Mittagessens schäkerten Vater und Krähenfuss miteinander. Mutter schaute ihnen mit feuchten Augen zu. Sie presste ihre Lippen zu einem dünnen Strich zusammen und suchte meinen Arm den sie zitternd umklammerte.

Krähenfuss holte ihre Pelze. Der baumelnde Kopf eines Fuchses grinste mich schräg an. Vater wartete im Schlitten, und sie rutschte eng an ihn heran. Er

fuhr eine Probefahrt um den Gasthof, und dann
verschwanden sie in einer Schneewolke.

Kleine Lawinen rutschten über den steilen Abhang
in die Schlucht.

Der Schlitten raste den Berg hinunter. Holzstecken,
tief vergraben im Schnee, markierten den Weg. An
einer steilen Kurve schlingerte das Gefährt. Der
untere Teil, da wo die Strasse der Forstverwaltung
begann, war vermutlich gepflügt worden und
vereist. Das Geheul des Motors hallte an den Felsen
wieder. Vater versuchte am Strassenrand zu
stoppen aber er geriet nur noch mehr in Fahrt.

Schreckensbleich..., nein, wahnsinnig vor Freude,
sah ich wie der Schlitten, Pelze, Beine und Arme
durch die Luft wirbelten und im schwarzen Rachen
der Schlucht verschwanden. Ich drehte mich um
und sah Mutter hinter mir. Sie runzelte die Stirn
aber dann entspannte sich ihr Gesicht. Ihr Mund
verzog sich zu einem Lächeln das sie aber schnell
unterdrückte.

Lieber Charles, ich weiss, dass Du mich immer ermahnst, meine Schreiberei nicht unvermittelt zu beenden aber ich finde es schwer ausführlicher darüber zu berichten. Ich denke, dass Du Dir alles zusammenreimen kannst.

Wir sassen in der Stube und starrten auf die flackernden Kerzen am Weihnachtsbaum. Unser Wirt reichte Glühwein und Weihnachtsguetzli herum und machte sich Sorgen warum Krähenfuss und Vater noch nicht zurück waren. Die Hiobsbotschaft kam per Telefonanruf. Die Rettungsmannschaft hatte zwei Leichen in der Schlucht gefunden.

Nach diesem tragischen Ereignis fuhren wir zurück nach Zürich, und Mutter stellte einen Privatlehrer für mich ein. Während all dieser Jahre liess sie mich nicht aus den Augen, und seit ihrem Tod lebe ich mehr schlecht als recht als Einsiedler im alten Haus. Gefängnisse kommen in verschiedenen Arten.

Jedes Jahr reise ich nach Untersee und kehre im hiesigen Gasthof ein. Herr und Frau Trun hatten sich bald nach dem Unglück in den Ruhestand begeben. Im ehemaligen Gasthaus Obsee wohnt heute ein neuer Pächter mit seiner grossen Familie.

Ich habe mich entschlossen, dass dies meine letzte Weihnacht hier ist. Mein Rechtsanwalt ist instruiert, er wird sich mit Dir in Verbindung setzen.

Ich schaue von meinem Brief auf. Die Berge stehen drohend über mir. Ich kenn sie doch die zwei Gesichter die mich in ewiger Anschuldigung anblicken. Sie rufen mich zu sich.

Ich verbleibe mit herzlichen Grüssen,

Herbert

## Die Ernte

Johann lehnte sich an den Türpfosten seines Bauernhauses und schaute über das Tal. Schon seit geraumer Zeit verfolgte er einen schwarzen Punkt in der weissen Landschaft, der allmählich näher kam und die Form eines Mannes annahm. Mühsam kämpfte sich dieser durch den tiefen Schnee.

Als er über die Hügelkuppe kletterte, sah Johann, dass er in seiner linken Hand ein braunes Couvert hielt und mit der rechten einen Spazierstock umklammerte. Hie und da rutschte er aus, zog sich aber sofort am Stock hoch und stapfte weiter. Er war von oben bis unten in Jägergrün gekleidet und seine Beine formten ein fast perfektes O.

Johann strich durch die Mähne seines Haares und tupfte sich mit einem karierten Nastuch den Schweiss von der Stirne. Dass der Bürgermeister sich höchstpersönlich zu ihm hinauf bemühte konnte nichts Gutes heissen.

Als der Bürgermeister Johann in der Tür stehen sah,
lüftete er den Hut und Johann beugte seinen Kopf
in übertriebener Unterwürfigkeit, gab sich dann
aber schnell einen Schupf, zog sich in die Höhe und
verschränkte die Arme.

„He ume, was wollt Ihr hier oben? Sicher nüd
Gfreuts."

Der Bürgermeister hustete sich einen Pfropfen
Schleim aus dem Hals und spuckte ihn in hohem
Bogen auf den Vorplatz.

„He nei, häsch rächt." Er zeigte auf das braune
Couvert. „Das ist die Kündigung für das Heimetli."
Er tat einen Schritt zurück und zeigte mit dem
Wanderstecken auf das verwitterte Chalet mit
überhängendem Dach und in Richtung Stall und
Felder. „Es tut mir leid und das so kurz vor
Weihnachten."

Von unter buschigen Augenbrauen inspizierte
Johann das Couvert und drehte es auf alle Seiten.
„Meinsch öppa, die wollen uns rauswerfen?"

Der Bürgermeister scharrte mit seinen genagelten Schuhen im Schnee. „Ja, dänk scho. Dein Pächter, de jung Schnufer, will das Geld und hat die Liegenschaft einem reichen Herrn verkauft. Einem richtig vornehmen Mann aus der Stadt, hat er mir gesagt. Er will das Haus renovieren lassen und  hier mit seiner Familie zur Erholung kommen."

Der Bürgermeister hob seinen Hut und schwenkte ihn. „Ich muss mich auf den Weg machen, es wird langsam dunkel."

Johanns griff sich an sein wild pochendes Herz. Bald würde er obdachlos sein, obdachlos mit Frau und fünf Kindern. Im Gang schaute er hinauf auf den Holzbalken mit den geschnitzten Zahlen. Dreissig Tage, das war genau so lang wie sie noch hier wohnen konnten.

Er legte das Couvert auf den Küchentisch und rieb sich die Hände an seinen Manchesterhosen, als ob der Brief giftig wäre.

Noch am gleichen Abend setzte sich seine Frau
Grete an den Stubentisch. Das Licht zweier
Adventskerzen umrahmte ihr rotes Haar wie einen
Heiligenschein. Sie tauchte den Federhalter in die
Tinte und ihre schwieligen Hände zitterten, als sie
getreulich schrieb, was ihr Johann vorsagte:

Sehr geehrter Herr,

ich bitte recht schön, dass wir noch ein bisschen in
unserem Haus bleiben können. So schnell können
wir nichts finden.

Gott segne Euch,

Johann


Am Heiligabend kam der Briefträger auf seinem
Moped über den gefrorenen Schnee geschlittert und
überbrachte einen Brief vom Herrn aus der Stadt.

Johann seufzte schwer. „Bis die nächste Ernte unter Dach ist, können wir bleiben. Aber dann müssen wir raus."

„Noch eine Ernte." Grete strich sich über die Stirne. „Noch eine Ernte", hallten die Stimmen der Kinder.

Sie sangen ein wehmütiges *Stille Nacht* unter dem bescheidenen Weihnachtsbaum. Johann schaute sich in der Stube um und fühlte sich urplötzlich besser; er blinzelte und lachte laut auf. He ja, das war ja gar nicht so schlecht, noch eine Ernte. Grete und die Kinder sahen ihn erstaunt an. Was hatte der Vater bloss zu lachen?

Die Dörfler schüttelten die Köpfe. Sie konnten nicht verstehen warum Johann pfeifend durch das Dorf marschierte.

„Sapperlot", sagten sie, „macht der sich überhaupt keine Sorgen?"

Und als Johann im Gasthaus eine Stange hinunterkippte und munter den letzten politischen

Stand mitdiskutierte, wollten sie es doch nun
endlich aus erster Quelle hören.

„Noch eine Ernte kannst bleiben, hat der
Bürgermeister gesagt? Solltest du nicht für ein
neues Heimetli schauen? Du weisst, wie schnell so
ein Sommer vergeht."

Johann schlug ihnen gutmütig auf die Schultern
und rieb sich den Nasenflügel. „Es wird sich dann
schon was zeigen."

Ende Januar fuhr Johann auf die Felder und
verteilte Gülle auf die Schneedecke. Die guten
Stoffe sickerten langsam auf den im Herbst
umgeackerten Boden.

Der Schnee fing an zu schmelzen. Es tropfte von
den Dachtraufen. Der Frühling war da, und die
Felder zeigten reiche braune Erde. Die Knospen
keimten an den Bäumen. Die Schneeglöckchen
bohrten ihre grünen Stengel durch den harten
Boden und durch das kurze Grass.

Johann tuckerte mit seinem Traktor in den nächsten Marktflecken unten im Tal. In der Landwirtschaftlichen Genossenschaft verhandelte er lange mit dem Chef bis er einen günstigen Preis für die Saat ergattern konnte.

Auf dem Heimweg raste er mit hoher Geschwindigkeit durch Untersee und hinterliess eine grosse Staubwolke. Auf dem Anhänger lagen drei prallvolle Jutesäcke.

Nur noch selten kam Johann zur Ruhe. Neben der Arbeit mit den Kühen und Schweinen pflanzte er nun jeden einzelnen Samen von Hand, fein säuberlich, in einem Finger Tiefe und einer Hand Abstand.

Dann kam das Hacken; jeden Tag hackte Johann seine steilen Felder, nicht einem Unkraut war es erlaubt zu überleben. Und er installierte eine ausgetüftelte Bewässerungsanlage mit Hilfe von alten Schläuchen, die er zusammengebettelt hatte und dem Wasser vom kleinen See.

Im Juni schnauften die Dörfler den Hang hinauf und schauten sich auf den Aeckern um. Auf und nieder gingen sie, schön den Rand entlang, aber sie sahen nichts als braune Erde.

„Da gibt's nichts zu sehen. Es isch öppä alles verreckt", teilten sie den Daheimgebliebenen mit.

Im August kamen sie wieder, die Dörfler, und fanden, dass kleine Keimlinge aus der Erde guckten. Aber die waren so klein und so gering, kaum der Rede wert.

Ein wundervoller Sommer wurde von einem noch schöneren Herbst abgelöst.

Und dann kamen die Novemberstürme und brachten den Herrn von der Stadt mitsamt seiner Frau. Er fuhr mit seinem nigelnagelneuen Mercedes den steilen Berghang hinauf. Schotter prasselte auf den makellosen Lack des vornehmen Autos. Es tönte wie Schüsse. Er parkierte, und sie gingen den Rest des Weges zu Fuss. Auf und nieder gingen sie, hin und her. Der Mann kratzte sich am Bart und reinigte seine Brillengläser. War das alles, diese kleinen verkümmerten Schösslinge. Die Frau lehnte sich schwer an ihren Mann und streckte den abgebrochenen Absatz eines ihrer Stöckelschuhe wie einen Dolch von sich. Beide schüttelten die Köpfe und die Frau starrte auf das Bauernhaus und murmelte: „Was, hier soll ich in die Ferien kommen?"

Weihnachten kam und ging. Die Keimlinge waren unter tiefem Schnee begraben. Hie und da ging Johann auf seine Felder, grub ein kleines Loch und schaute seine Pflänzchen liebevoll an.

Um Überleben zu können arbeitete Johann im Sägewerk und Grete ging im Gasthof in Untersee servieren.

Im Januar koppelte Johann das Güllenfass an seinen Traktor und fuhr wieder auf die Felder. Sein kleinster Sohn, der auf seinem Schoss sass, jauchzte, als die Gülle die wunderbarsten Muster auf den Schnee zeichnete. Der Wind und das Wetter taten ihre Arbeit, der Schnee schmolz langsam und wieder sickerte die Gülle hinunter und nährte die Sämlinge.

Der Frühling kam. Der Schnee gab hunderte von Pflänzchen frei. Ja, sicher, sie waren klein, aber gesund.

Schon bald war es wieder Sommer. Die Dörfler kamen auf ihren Inspektionsgang. Sie sahen wohl kleine pyramidenartige Schösslinge, schüttelten aber die Köpfe. Was war ächt das nur?

Als sie Johann fragten, schmunzelte er nur geheimnisvoll. Grete, die jeden Sonntag zur Kirche ging, zog sich nach der Messe das Kopftuch fester um ihre roten Haare und eilte heimwärts, ohne etwas preiszugeben. Die zwei grösseren, schulpflichtigen Kinder wurden von den Flegelbuben mit Schlägen bedroht wenn sie nicht endlich mit der Wahrheit rausrückten. Die beiden blieben stumm. Und der Chef der landwirtschaftlichen Genossenschaft machte eine Reisverschlussbewegung über seinen Mund.

Advent kam und Johann und seine Familie freuten sich auf die zweite Weihnacht ihrer Gnadenfrist. Sie waren nicht überrascht als sie einen Brief vom Herrn aus der Stadt erhielten. Er schrieb, dass seine Geduld bald am Ende sei und, dass er nicht für ewig warten wolle. Was immer sie auch angepflanzt hätten, sollte doch bald so weit sein.

Auf Geheiss von Johann antwortete Grete wieder, diesmal beim Kerzenlicht einer Adventskerze.

Sehr geehrter Herr,

es tut mir aufrichtig leid, dass die Ernte so lang hat, bis sie unter Dach und Fach ist, und dass Ihr unser Heimetli nicht endlich übernehmen könnt. Bevor es zu schneien begann, dünnte ich die Sämlinge aus, welche ich vor zirka zwei Jahren pflanzen tat. Ich habe nun über eintausend  starke Pflanzen. Unsere Weihnachtsbäume können, so Gott es will, in ein paar Jahren geerntet werden. Ich habe nie gedacht, dass das so lange dauert. Aber vielleicht gebt Ihr uns noch ein bisschen Zeit, es kann nicht gejufelt werden.

Besten Dank und frohe Weihnachten.

Johann

Vier lange Wochen hörten sie nichts. Am Heiligabend kämpfte sich der Briefträger mit seinem Moped durch den tiefen Schnee und brachte die Antwort.

Johann starrte auf den Brief, er schluckte trocken, reckte den Kopf und klemmte seine Daumen unter die Hosenträger und fing an zu tanzen. „He ume den, er schreibt, dass wir bleiben können, so lange wir wollen, er kapiert's." Er nahm Grete in die Arme und schwang sie rum. Die Kinder klammerten sich an die Beine ihrer Eltern und tanzten mit.

Als Johann eine kleine Verschnaufpause einlegte, fuhr er fort, „Jetzt losid mol, der Herr sagt, dass seine Frau sich für eine Villa in Spanien entschieden habe, so ein Haus, wo sich die Hasen und Füchse gute Nacht sagen, hat ja nur Nachteile. Wir müssen nicht pressieren."

Die ganze Familie tanzte noch ein Polka durch die Stube, während unter dem Schnee die kleinen Tännchen geduldig auf zukünftige Weihnachten warteten.

Printed in Great Britain
by Amazon